Graphic Dickens

DAVID COPPERFIELD

Retold by Hilary Burningham
Illustrated by Chris Rowlatt

READZNE

ReadZone Books Limited

50 Godfrey Avenue
Twickenham
TW2 7PF

For Celia

British Library Cataloguing in Publication Data (CIP) is available for this title.

Printed in Great Britain by Ashford Colour Press Ltd, Gosport

ISBN 978 1 78322 012 0

Visit our website: www.readzonebooks.com

HERE BEGINS MY STORY.
MY NAME IS DAVID COPPERFIELD.
MY FATHER, ALSO NAMED
DAVID COPPERFIELD,
DIED SIX MONTHS BEFORE I WAS BORN,
LEAVING MY MOTHER ALONE
AND PREGNANT.

ABOUT THE TIME I WAS DUE TO BE BORN, A VISITOR ARRIVED AT OUR COTTAGE.

Mrs David Copperfield, I think? I am Miss Betsey Trotwood, your late husband's aunt.

Please come in, Miss Trotwood.

I have no doubt your child will be a girl, and I intend to be her godmother. I would like you to name her Betsey Trotwood Copperfield.

But the baby might be a b-.

AT THAT MOMENT, OUR SERVANT, PEGGOTTY, CAME IN WITH THE TEA THINGS.

Oh, oh.

My dear Mrs Copperfield, it's starting. Let's get you upstairs.

SOME HOURS LATER THE DOCTOR, WHO HAD BEEN UPSTAIRS WITH MY MOTHER, CAME DOWN.

Girl? No, it's a boy.

And how is the baby, the baby girl?

A boy? Never! I'm not having that! Goodbye!

3

FOR SEVERAL YEARS, THE THREE OF US, MY MOTHER, PEGGOTTY AND I, WERE VERY HAPPY TOGETHER IN OUR PRETTY COTTAGE.

BUT ONE DAY, MY MOTHER BROUGHT HOME A NEW FRIEND. HIS NAME WAS MR. MURDSTONE...

I hope you have had a very pleasant evening, ma'am.

A **very** pleasant evening, thank you, Peggotty.

Come! Let us be the best friends in the world! Shake hands with me, David.

AT FIRST MR. MURDSTONE WAS VERY NICE. ONE DAY, HE TOOK ME TO THE SEASIDE.

Master Davy, should you like to spend a fortnight with me, at my brother's at Yarmouth?

Don't worry, she's going to stay with friends too.

That would be lovely, Peggotty, but what about mother? She can't live by herself.

Then yes, please. Yes!

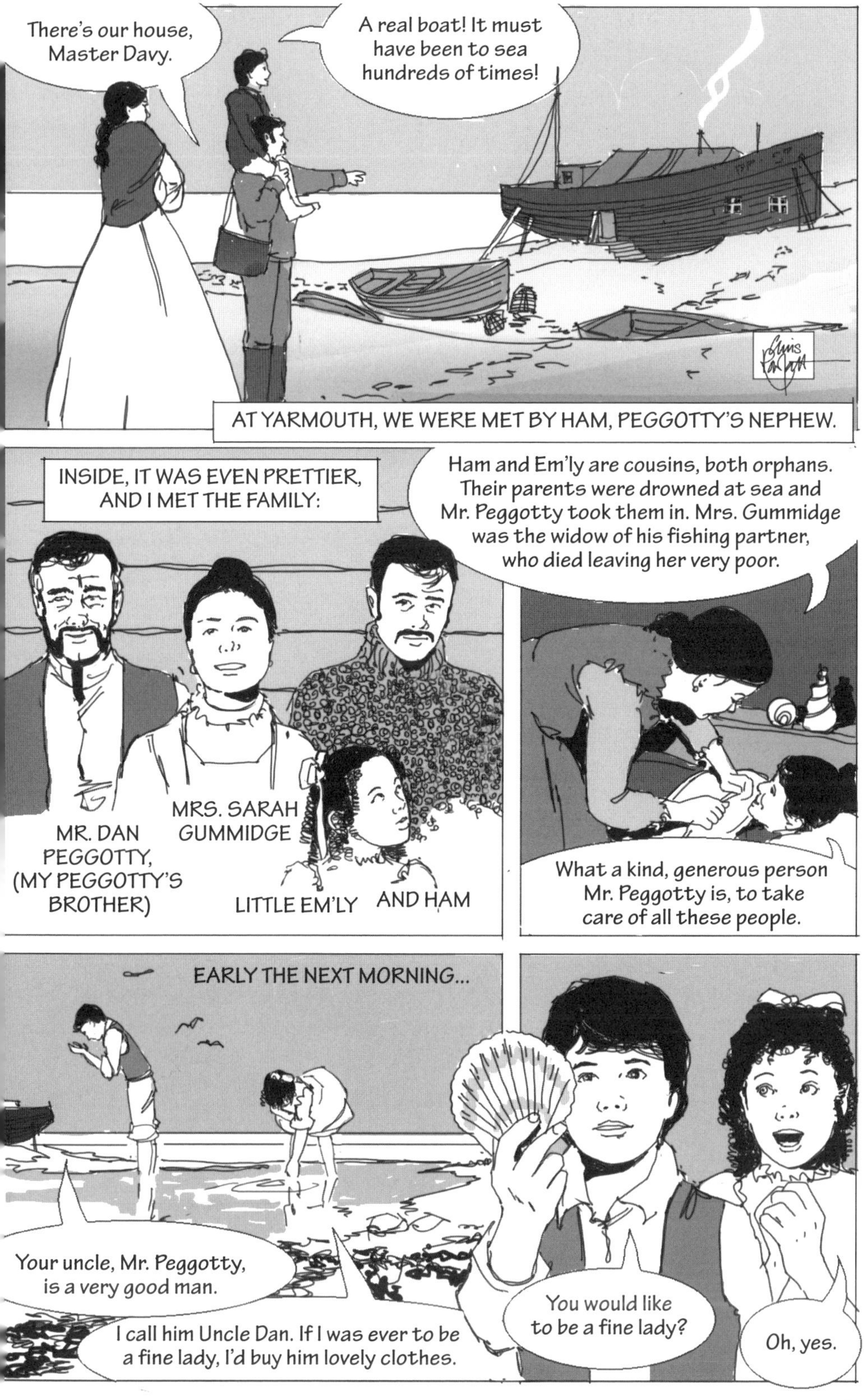

There's our house, Master Davy.
A real boat! It must have been to sea hundreds of times!
AT YARMOUTH, WE WERE MET BY HAM, PEGGOTTY'S NEPHEW.
INSIDE, IT WAS EVEN PRETTIER, AND I MET THE FAMILY:
Ham and Em'ly are cousins, both orphans. Their parents were drowned at sea and Mr. Peggotty took them in. Mrs. Gummidge was the widow of his fishing partner, who died leaving her very poor.
MR. DAN PEGGOTTY, (MY PEGGOTTY'S BROTHER)
MRS. SARAH GUMMIDGE
LITTLE EM'LY
AND HAM
What a kind, generous person Mr. Peggotty is, to take care of all these people.
EARLY THE NEXT MORNING...
Your uncle, Mr. Peggotty, is a very good man.
I call him Uncle Dan. If I was ever to be a fine lady, I'd buy him lovely clothes.
You would like to be a fine lady?
Oh, yes.

OF COURSE I FELL IN LOVE WITH LITTLE EM'LY.

Lor! Ain't it beautiful?

Yes, indeed.

SOMETIMES, MRS. GUMMIDGE FELT VERY SORRY FOR HERSELF.

I'm a lone, lone creature and everything goes against me.

There, there, Sarah Gummidge, cheer up.

SOON IT WAS TIME TO GO HOME. I COULDN'T WAIT TO SEE MY MOTHER, BUT PEGGOTTY TOOK ME INTO THE KITCHEN.

Peggotty, why have we come into the kitchen? Where is Mama?

Master Davy, I should have told you before. You have got a new pa. Come and meet him.

Now, Clara, remember – control yourself and the boy. Always control.

I WAS GIVEN A DIFFERENT, SMALLER ROOM, FAR AWAY FROM MAMA'S.

THERE WAS A NEW MAID, AND A BIG NEW FIERCE DOG THAT DIDN'T LIKE ME.

NEXT, MR. MURDSTONE'S SISTER, MISS JANE MURDSTONE, CAME TO STAY WITH US.

Now Clara, my dear, I am here to help you in every possible way. Please give me your keys, and I'll attend to the household in future.

MAMA, OF COURSE, HAD TO GIVE HER THE KEYS.

LIFE IN THE COTTAGE BECAME MORE AND MORE UNPLEASANT, BUT I DISCOVERD MY FATHER'S BOOKS IN A LITTLE SPARE ROOM. I READ AND READ WHENEVER I COULD.

ONE DAY, WHEN I COULDN'T DO MY LESSONS, MR. MURDSTONE TOOK ME UPSTAIRS AND PICKED UP A CANE.

Come, Davy. Try once more. You can do this.

Clara, be firm with the boy. He has not learned his lessons.

He has not!

EVERY MORNING I DID MY LESSONS WITH MAMA. THE MURDSTONES INSISTED ON WATCHING, WHICH MADE ME FRIGHTENED AND CONFUSED.

Oh, don't! Pray don't beat me! I can't learn with you and Miss Murdstone there. I can't!

Can't you indeed, David? We'll see about that.

Why you little ...! I'll teach you a lesson!

TERRIFIED, I BIT HIS HAND – HARD!

Take **that**! And **that**! And **that**!

Help! Help! Aaaargh!

7

THE MURDSTONES KEPT ME IN MY ROOM FOR A WEEK, AND THEN I WAS SENT AWAY TO SCHOOL.

Goodbye, Davy. You will come home in the holidays and be a better boy.

Good, Clara. Be firm.

I forgive you, my dear boy. God bless you!

Clara, that is enough!

A SHORT DISTANCE DOWN THE ROAD, THE DRIVER STOPPED THE CART.

Here, Davy, some cakes for you, and a bit of money from your mother and me.

Have one of Peggotty's cakes. She makes all our cakes and does the cooking.

BARKIS
CARRIER

Hmmm! They're very good. Perhaps when you're writing to her, you'll tell her that Barkis is willin'.

8

Come, don't you fidget. Your bones are younger than mine.

BARKIS LEFT ME AT AN INN, WHERE I WAS PUT ON THE LONDON COACH. I WAS SQUASHED AND UNCOMFORTABLE.

I WAS GLAD WHEN WE *GOT* TO LONDON. A MAN HAD COME TO MEET ME.

You're the new boy? I'm Mr. Mell, one of the masters at Salem House, your new school.

ALMSHOUSES FOR POOR & NEEDY WOMEN

There's someone here who will cook your food and give you some milk.

My Charley!

Can you cook this young gentleman's breakfast for him?

Of course.

That must be his mother.

SALEM HOUSE

AT LAST WE REACHED THE SCHOOL.

A MAN WITH A WOODEN LEG OPENED THE DOOR. I LATER LEARNED THAT HIS NAME WAS TUNGAY.

Poor Mr. Mell. The boots he's wearing are pretty bad, too.

Cobbler's been, Mr. Mell. He can't mend your boots. They're past mending.

NEXT, MR. MELL SHOWED ME THE SCHOOLROOM. THE OTHER BOYS HADN'T COME BACK TO SCHOOL YET.

What are you doing up there?

Beware of him He Bites

I beg your pardon, sir. If you please, I'm looking for the dog.

I'm very sorry, Copperfield. My instructions are to pin this on your back.

Because I bit Mr. Murdstone!

A FEW DAYS LATER, THE BOYS RETURNED TO SCHOOL --- AND SO DID MR. CREAKLE, THE HEADMASTER.

I have the pleasure of knowing your stepfather, Copperfield. He knows me and I know him.

If you please, sir, if I might be allowed to take off this writing --- before I meet the other boys?

NEXT I MET TOMMY TRADDLES AND SOME OF THE OTHER BOYS.

Hey, Towzer!

Look here! Here's a game!

Lie down!

NO, definitely NOT, sir!

THEN I MET STEERFORTH, A SENIOR. HE WAS VERY NICE TO ME.

I say Copperfield, it's a jolly shame, having to wear that sign. By the way, have you any money?

Don't worry, young Copperfield, I'll take care of you.

You're very kind.

WITH THE LAST OF THE MONEY FROM MY MOTHER AND PEGGOTTY, STEERFORTH BOUGHT CURRANT WINE AND CAKES TO HAVE LATER.

THE NEXT DAY, SCHOOL BEGAN IN EARNEST.

Skeletons, Traddles? What nonsense! Stop it at once.

What do you think of this for a tooth Copperfield? Take off that sign. It gets in my way.

STEERFORTH SOMETIMES HAD TROUBLE SLEEPING. TO HELP HIM SLEEP, I USED TO TELL HIM THE STORIES I HAD READ IN MY FATHER'S BOOKS AT HOME.

And then what happened David?

Just a minute. I'll remember...

ONE DAY, MR. MELL WAS LEFT ON HIS OWN WITH THE BOYS.

SILENCE! Silence I say! Please sit down Mr. Steerforth.

Sit down yourself and mind your own business.

You are a favourite here. How dare you insult a gentleman...!

A gentleman? Where? I don't see a gentleman. YOU are no better than a beggar.

What's all this talk of favourites? And beggars?

He accused me of being a favourite. I said he's a beggar. If he isn't, a very close relative is.

That's my fault. I told Steerforth about Mr.Mell's mother in the almshouse.

There is no favouritism here, Mr. Mell. Go, if you please. The sooner the better.

James Steerforth, I hope you live to be ashamed of what you have done this day.

I FELT VERY SORRY FOR MR. MELL. WHY HAD STEERFORTH TREATED HIM SO BADLY?

| ONE DAY I HAD VISITORS | JUST THEN, STEERFORTH HAPPENED TO WALK BY. |

We brung you some treats. Mrs. Gummidge boiled them up for you.

Steerforth, if you please, these are two Yarmouth boatmen, relatives of my nurse. Ham, Mr. Peggotty, Mr. Steerforth has been very kind to me.

Why, thank you. And how is dear, dear Peggotty?

You mustn't praise me so, David. How are you both?

You must come to see us if you're ever in Yarmouth, Mr. Steerforth!

AT LAST THE TERM WAS OVER AND I WAS IN BARKIS'S CART ON MY WAY HOME TO BLUNDERSTONE.

Well, I'm still waiting for an answer. So will you tell her, Barkis is waiting for an answer.

I gave your message. I wrote to Peggotty saying, Barkis is willing.

AT HOME THERE WAS A NEW ARRIVAL.

He is your brother, Davy, my pretty boy! Look, his eyes are just like yours.

You are a fool, Clara. How could you compare my brother's baby and that boy?

The boy is not to touch the baby, Clara. Be firm!

But Edward ...

That is enough, Clara.

EVEN THOUGH IT MEANT LEAVING MY MOTHER AND BABY BROTHER, I WAS GLAD WHEN IT WAS TIME TO GO BACK TO SCHOOL.

13

NO! Oh no!

I have something to tell you my child. Your mama was dangerously ill. She is now dead.

Master Copperfield? I am Mr. Omer, the undertaker. Please come with me, I am to measure you for a black suit.

I LEFT SALEM HOUSE THE NEXT AFTERNOON.

AT YARMOUTH, I LOOKED FOR BARKIS, BUT HE WASN'T THERE.

Do you know how my little brother is, sir?

I'm so sorry, my boy. He is in his mother's arms. The baby is dead.

AT HOME PEGGOTTY GREETED ME WITH A WARM HUG.

Did you bring your shirts?

Yes, ma'am. I have brought home all my clothes.

MR. MURDSTONE TOOK NO NOTICE OF ME AT ALL.

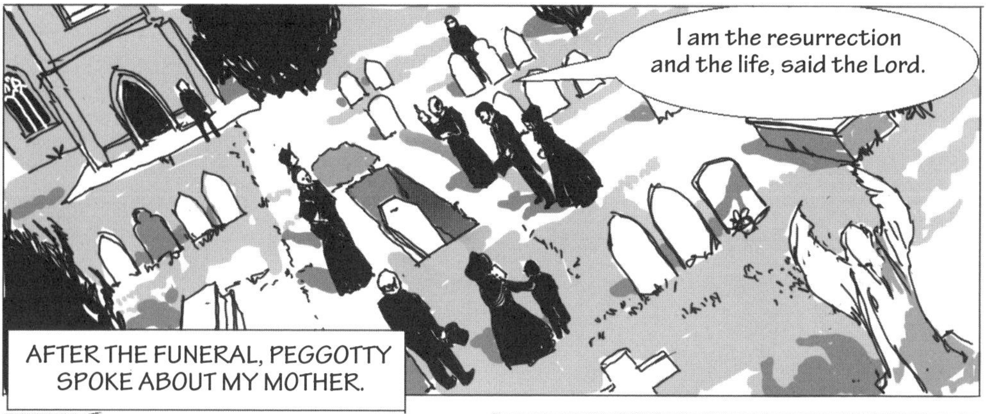
I am the resurrection and the life, said the Lord.
AFTER THE FUNERAL, PEGGOTTY SPOKE ABOUT MY MOTHER.

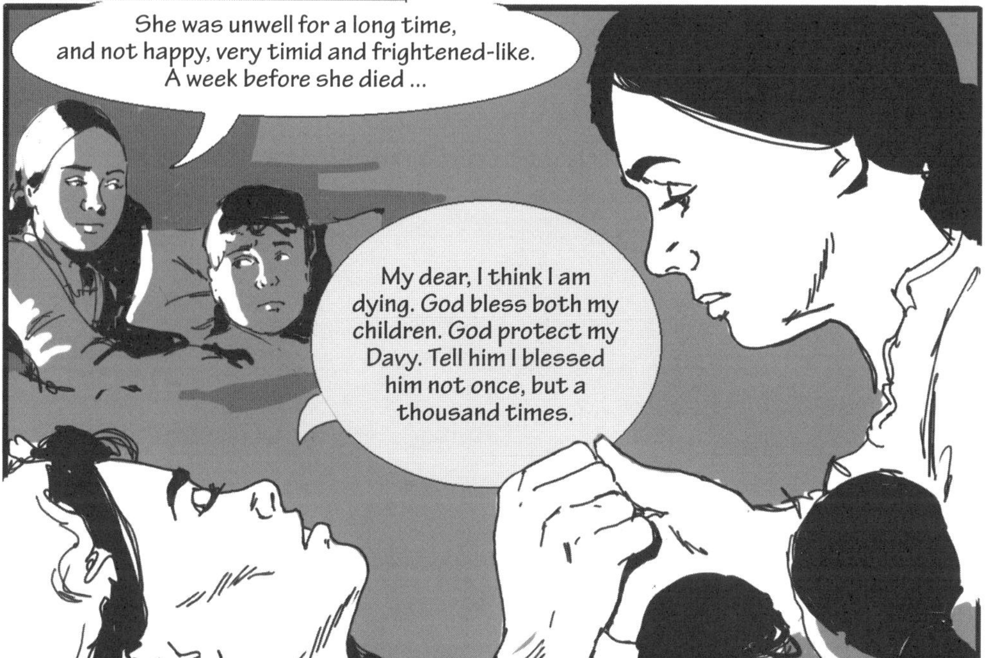
She was unwell for a long time, and not happy, very timid and frightened-like. A week before she died ...
My dear, I think I am dying. God bless both my children. God protect my Davy. Tell him I blessed him not once, but a thousand times.
She died like a child that had gone to sleep.

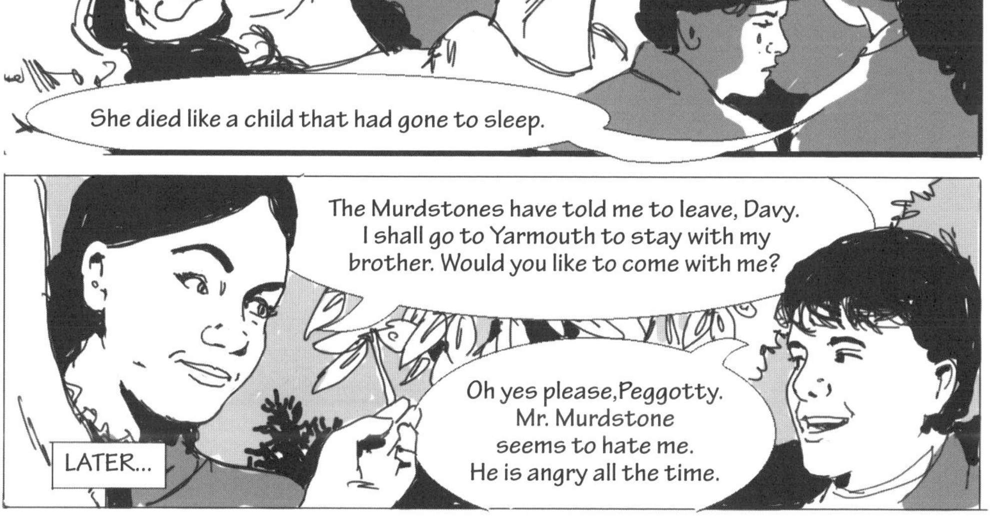
LATER...
The Murdstones have told me to leave, Davy. I shall go to Yarmouth to stay with my brother. Would you like to come with me?
Oh yes please,Peggotty. Mr. Murdstone seems to hate me. He is angry all the time.

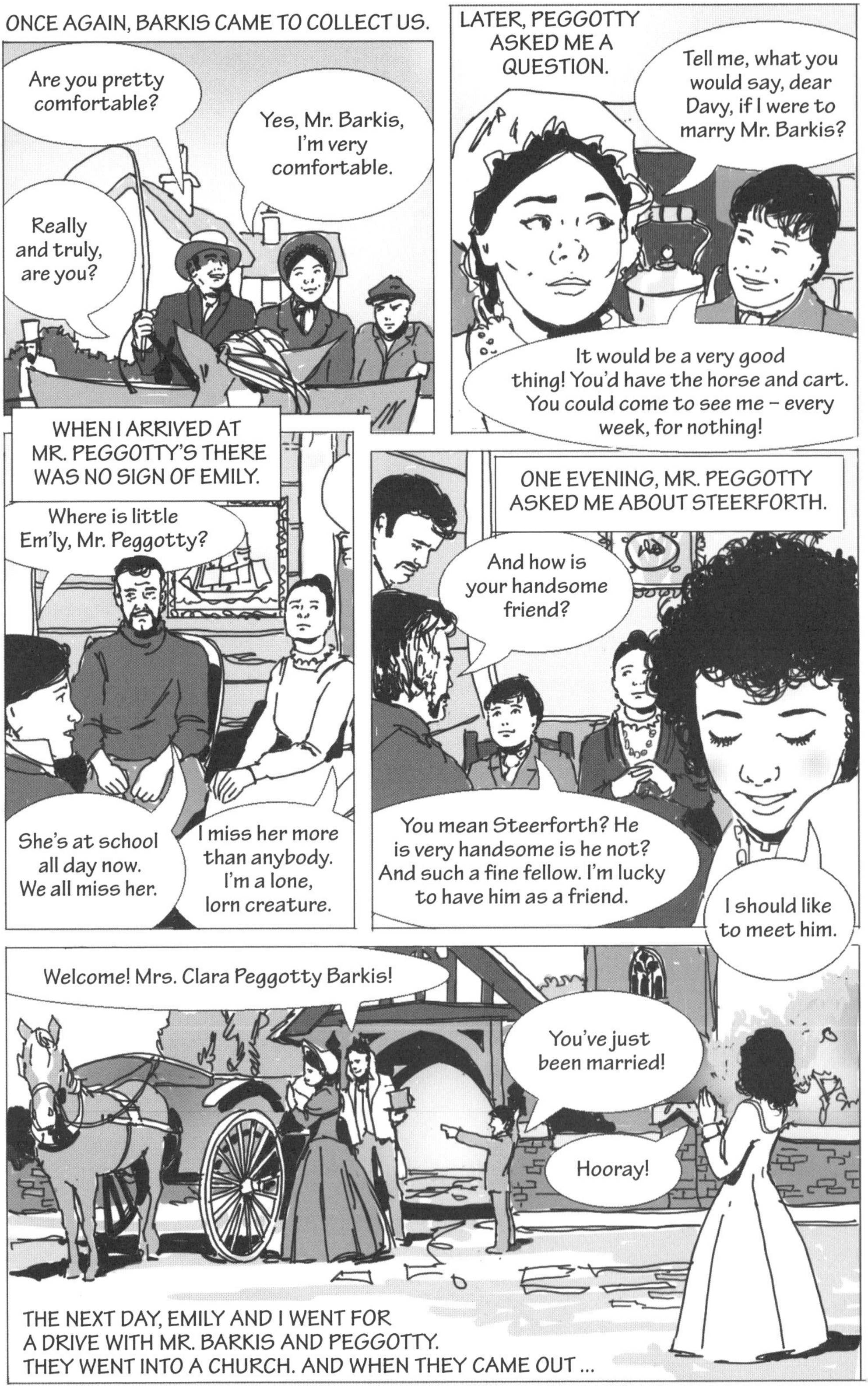
ONCE AGAIN, BARKIS CAME TO COLLECT US.
Are you pretty comfortable?
Yes, Mr. Barkis, I'm very comfortable.
Really and truly, are you?
LATER, PEGGOTTY ASKED ME A QUESTION.
Tell me, what you would say, dear Davy, if I were to marry Mr. Barkis?
It would be a very good thing! You'd have the horse and cart. You could come to see me – every week, for nothing!
WHEN I ARRIVED AT MR. PEGGOTTY'S THERE WAS NO SIGN OF EMILY.
Where is little Em'ly, Mr. Peggotty?
She's at school all day now. We all miss her.
I miss her more than anybody. I'm a lone, lorn creature.
ONE EVENING, MR. PEGGOTTY ASKED ME ABOUT STEERFORTH.
And how is your handsome friend?
You mean Steerforth? He is very handsome is he not? And such a fine fellow. I'm lucky to have him as a friend.
I should like to meet him.
Welcome! Mrs. Clara Peggotty Barkis!
You've just been married!
Hooray!
THE NEXT DAY, EMILY AND I WENT FOR A DRIVE WITH MR. BARKIS AND PEGGOTTY. THEY WENT INTO A CHURCH. AND WHEN THEY CAME OUT ...

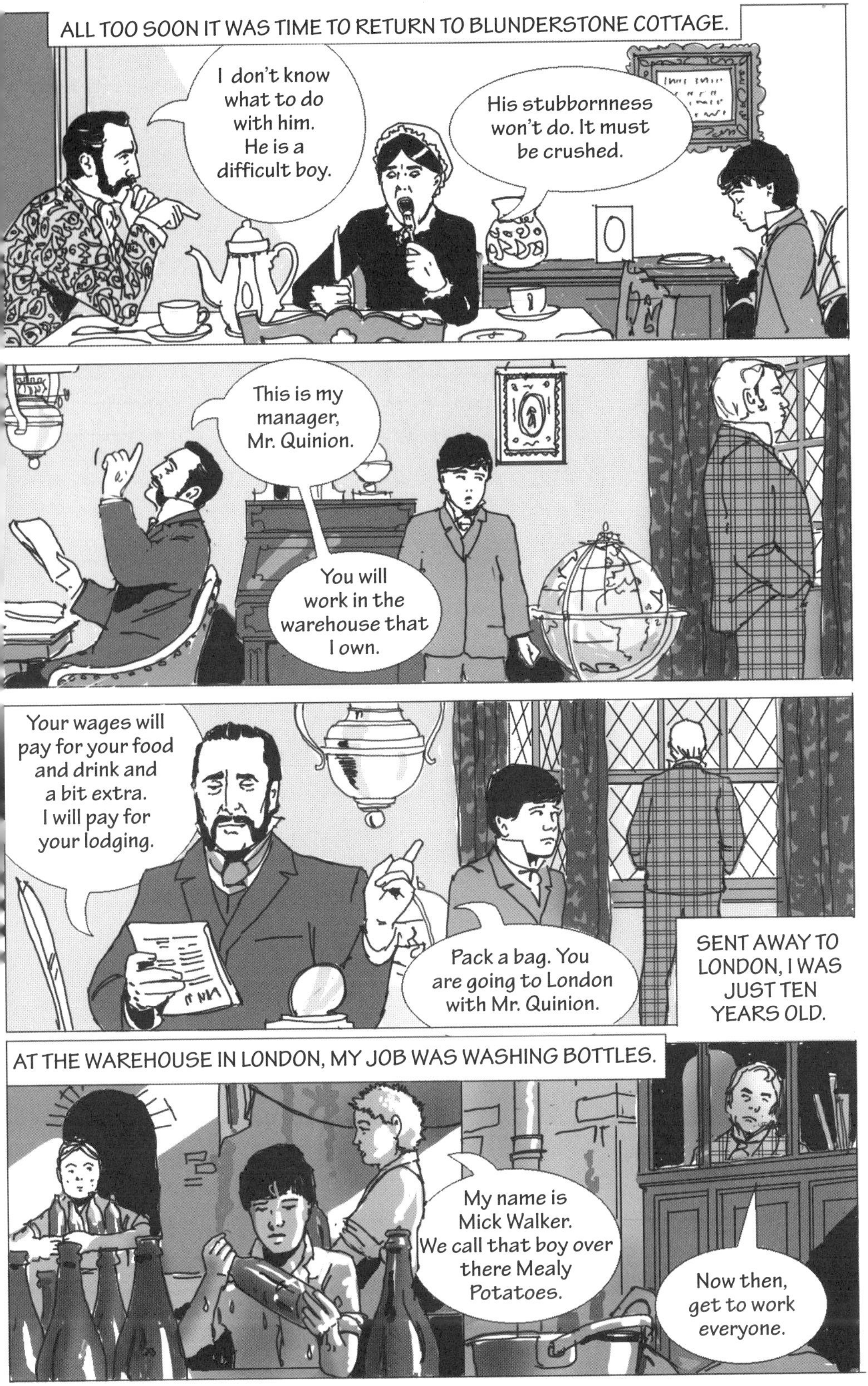
ALL TOO SOON IT WAS TIME TO RETURN TO BLUNDERSTONE COTTAGE.
I don't know what to do with him. He is a difficult boy.
His stubbornness won't do. It must be crushed.
This is my manager, Mr. Quinion.
You will work in the warehouse that I own.
Your wages will pay for your food and drink and a bit extra. I will pay for your lodging.
Pack a bag. You are going to London with Mr. Quinion.
SENT AWAY TO LONDON, I WAS JUST TEN YEARS OLD.
AT THE WAREHOUSE IN LONDON, MY JOB WAS WASHING BOTTLES.
My name is Mick Walker. We call that boy over there Mealy Potatoes.
Now then, get to work everyone.

THAT SAME EVENING MR. QUINION INVITED ME INTO HIS OFFICE.

Copperfield, this is Mr. Micawber. He will receive you as a lodger.

Master Copperfield, I hope you are well, sir? Allow me to show you the way to my abode.

My dear, our new lodger. He is to have the room on the top floor.

Oh dear. I never thought I should have to take in a lodger.

MR. MICAWBER SEEMED TO OWE MONEY TO A LOT OF PEOPLE, WHO WERE ALWAYS TRYING TO COLLECT IT.

Come! Pay us will you? I mended them boots a month ago.

Just pay us. D'ye hear?

To us, my dear, I'm sure something will turn up soon.

BUT SOMEHOW, THEY BOUGHT FOOD AND DRINK, ESPECIALLY DRINK

SOMETIMES, MR. MICAWBER WOULD GIVE ME THINGS TO TAKE TO THE PAWNBROKER TO EXCHANGE FOR A FEW PENCE.

I'm sorry, son. They're not worth very much.

ONE DAY, MR. MICAWBER WAS ARRESTED FOR NOT PAYING HIS BILLS. I VISITED HIM IN PRISON.

I tell you Davy, if a man has an income of twenty pounds and spends nineteen pounds, ninety-nine pence, he will be happy, but if he spends twenty pounds and ten pence, he will be miserable.

MRS. MICAWBER AND THE CHILDREN ALSO MOVED INTO THE PRISON. FRIENDS BROUGHT THEM GIFTS OF FOOD.

LOCKED UP IN PRISON, MR. MICAWBER COULD NOT EARN ANY MONEY TO PAY HIS BILLS. HE DECIDED TO PRESENT A PETITION. ALL THE OTHER PRISONERS SIGNED IT.

AFTER PRESENTING HIS PETITION IN COURT, HE WAS SET FREE.

May I ask, Mrs. Micawber, what you and Mr. Micawber intend to do, now that he is out of prison?

We will go to my family in Plymouth, to be ready when something turns up.

LATER...

I COULD NOT IMAGINE LIVING IN LONDON WITHOUT THE MICAWBERS, I WROTE TO PEGGOTTY ASKING HER FOR THE ADDRESS OF MY AUNT, MISS BETSEY TROTWOOD.

I FINISHED MY WEEK'S WORK, THEN PAID A BOY WITH A CART TO TAKE MY TRUNK TO THE COACH STATION. BUT –

All my things – and the money Peggotty sent me.

Stop! Stop thief!

I'll report you to the police. You're a runaway.

Peggotty writes that Miss Betsey lives near Dover, but she's not sure where. She's sent me some money. Dear Peggotty.

I SET OFF TO WALK TO DOVER. BUT I HAD LEARNED SOMETHING FROM THE MICAWBERS.

MY MONEY FOR THE JOURNEY WAS GONE.

Will you give me eighteen pence for this?

Half that. I'll give you nine pence. Take it or leave it.

ON THE SIXTH DAY, I REACHED DOVER.

Excuse me, I'm looking for Miss Betsey Trotwood.

You'd better follow me. I work for her.

Go away! Go along! No boys here!

If you please, Aunt, I am your nephew.

EH?

TO MY SURPRISE, SHE SAT DOWN, HARD ON THE GARDEN PATH!

Oh, Lord!

Yes, I am David Copperfield. Since my dear mama died, I have been very badly treated and have run away to you.

Janet, go upstairs, to Mr. Dick and say I wish to speak to him.

You have heard me mention my late brother, David Copperfield?

Well this is his son. He has run away. The question is what shall I do with him?

Why if I was you, I should – I should wash him!

Janet, Mr. Dick speaks such good sense. Heat the bath!

Janet!

Donkeys! Come quickly!

AFTER THE DONKEY INCIDENT I HAD MY BATH, AFTER WHICH I WAS DRESSED IN A SHIRT AND TROUSERS OF MR. DICK AND WRAPPED UP IN TWO OR THREE OLD SHAWLS.

David, I have written to your stepfather.

Shall you send me back to him?

I can't say. We shall see.

NEXT, AUNT BETSEY SENT ME TO SEE HOW MR. DICK WAS GETTING ON WITH HIS MEMORIAL. A MEMORIAL WAS A KIND OF DIARY.

Aunt Betsey would like to know how you're getting on with the Memorial.

Please tell her I'm getting on very well indeed, but King Charles the First keeps getting into it.

What do you think of this kite? I made it myself. We'll go and fly it you and I. When it flies high it helps me sort out the facts.

Helps you sort out the facts? Yes of course, Mr. Dick.

Mr.Dick says he's getting on very well, Aunt Betsey. But tell me, is he a little bit crazy?

Not a bit. He has been called that. His own brother would have him locked away for the rest of his life, but I put a stop to it.

22

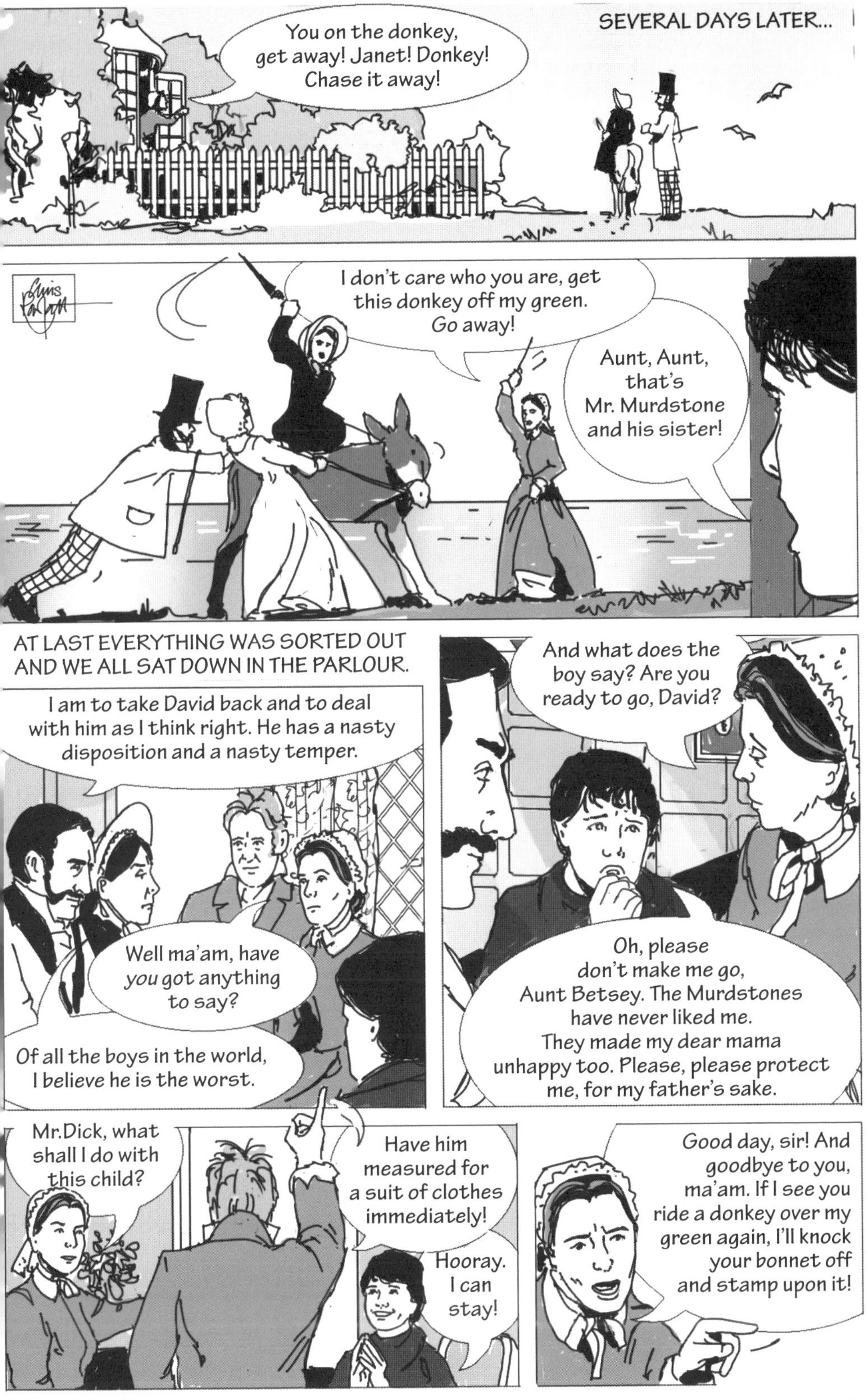
SEVERAL DAYS LATER...
You on the donkey, get away! Janet! Donkey! Chase it away!
I don't care who you are, get this donkey off my green. Go away!
Aunt, Aunt, that's Mr. Murdstone and his sister!
AT LAST EVERYTHING WAS SORTED OUT AND WE ALL SAT DOWN IN THE PARLOUR.
I am to take David back and to deal with him as I think right. He has a nasty disposition and a nasty temper.
Well ma'am, have you got anything to say?
Of all the boys in the world, I believe he is the worst.
And what does the boy say? Are you ready to go, David?
Oh, please don't make me go, Aunt Betsey. The Murdstones have never liked me. They made my dear mama unhappy too. Please, please protect me, for my father's sake.
Mr.Dick, what shall I do with this child?
Have him measured for a suit of clothes immediately!
Hooray. I can stay!
Good day, sir! And goodbye to you, ma'am. If I see you ride a donkey over my green again, I'll knock your bonnet off and stamp upon it!

SO BEGAN MY NEW LIFE. AUNT BETSEY CALLED ME TROTWOOD COPPERFIELD, BUT SOON SHORTENED IT TO 'TROT'.

Trot, we must not forget your education. Tomorrow we will go to Canterbury. You will meet Mr. Wickfield who knows about such things.

Is Mr. Wickfield at home, Uriah Heep?

Mr. Wickfield's at home, ma'am.

Mr. Wickfield, this is my adopted nephew. I want to put him in a good school, the best.

If you'll please to go inside.

The best school? You want the best? Come, I will show you the best school in Canterbury.

I WAITED IN MR. WICKFIELD'S OFFICE WHILE HE TOOK AUNT BETSEY TO SEE THE SCHOOL. WHEN THEY RETURNED ...

The school is very good indeed, Trot. I am sure you will do well there.

And you are welcome to stay here. This is an excellent house for study: it's quiet and there's plenty of room.

And this is my little housekeeper, my daughter Agnes. Her mother died many years ago.

Trot, be a credit to yourself, to me and to Mr. Dick, and Heaven be with you.

Thank you, again and again, dear Aunt, and send my love to Mr. Dick.

THE NEXT DAY I STARTED AT MY NEW SCHOOL. THE HEADMASTER WAS DR. STRONG. HE HAD A VERY PRETTY YOUNG WIFE NAMED ANNIE.

Dr. Strong, here is your new pupil, Trotwood Copperfield.

Good. Let's go to the schoolroom.

By the way, Wickfield, have you found a suitable position for my wife's cousin, Jack Maldon, yet?

No. Not yet.

I hope it can be done soon. Jack Maldon is out of work and lazy – a bad combination. A position abroad would be best.

DR. STRONG'S SCHOOL WAS VERY DIFFERENT FROM SALEM HOUSE. IT WAS STRANGE TO BE A SCHOOLBOY AGAIN.

Good morning, sir.

We have a new boy, gentlemen, Trotwood Copperfield.

THAT EVENING AS I DINED WITH MR. WICKFIELD, OUR DINNER WAS INTERRUPTED – BY MR. JACK MALDON.

Have you dined, sir? Will you join us?

It seems I am being sent abroad – to India. I am being banished, even though my cousin Annie said she liked to have her friends close by.

Thank you. I am dining with my cousin Annie. Goodbye!

EVERY NIGHT AFTER DINNER, AGNES PLAYED THE PIANO WHILE MR. WICKFIELD DRANK HIS WINE. HE DRANK RATHER A LOT OF WINE.

DOWNSTAIRS, URIAH HEEP WORKED LATE.

You are working late tonight, Uriah.

ALTHOUGH HE TRIED TO PLEASE ME I COULD NOT LIKE URIAH HEEP

I am reading, Master Copperfield, improving my knowledge.

THE NIGHT BEFORE JACK MALDON LEFT FOR INDIA, DR. STRONG AND HIS YOUNG WIFE ANNIE GAVE A GOING-AWAY PARTY FOR HIM.

Lovely, Annie, lovely.

Farewell, Mr. Jack. Here's to your success abroad.

Why, Annie, my dear. You have lost the bow from your dress.

Never mind, Mother. It doesn't matter.

AFTER JACK MALDON HAD LEFT, ANNIE FELT UNWELL.

ONE AFTERNOON, I WENT TO TEA WITH URIAH HEEP AND HIS MOTHER.

'Umble we are, 'umble we have been, and 'umble we shall always be, Master Davy.

I wonder how soon I can leave!

JUST AT THAT MOMENT ...

Is it possible?

What an extraordinary meeting. Copperfield! How are you?

I am well, thanks. And may I present Mrs. Heep and her son. This is Mr. Micawber, an old friend from London.

We are just 'umble friends of Master Copperfield, sir. We are thankful for his company.

MICAWBER AND I LEFT TOGETHER AND WENT STRAIGHT AWAY TO THE INN WHERE HE WAS STAYING.

My dear, here's a surprise! Master Copperfield is a pupil at Dr. Strong's.

My dear Master Copperfield!

I thought you were at Plymouth, ma'am.

I will not hide from you, my dear, we were not warmly welcomed by my family. In short, nothing turned up. We are here seeking new opportunities.

LATER, LOOKING OUT OF MY WINDOW I SAW...

Well, well. What goes on here? What can Heep be up to?

THE NEXT NIGHT I DINED WITH THE MICAWBERS.

Copperfield, your friend Heep will go far. He may put some work my way.

I don't like the look of this. What work?

BUT THE NEXT MORNING I RECEIVED A LETTER FROM MICAWBER.

My dear young friend
All is over. There is no
hope. This is the last
communication you
will ever receive
From the beggared
outcast.
Wilkins Micawber

WALKING TO SCHOOL I SAW MR. AND MRS. MICAWBER LEAVING TOWN ON THE LONDON COACH.

BUT I HAD NO TIME TO WORRY ABOUT THE MICAWBERS.

MY SCHOOLDAYS WERE COMING TO AN END. I WAS SEVENTEEN AND HEAD BOY OF DR. STRONG'S SCHOOL.

I WAS IN LOVE AND OUT OF LOVE IN THOSE DAYS, BUT ALWAYS THERE, LIKE A SISTER, WAS AGNES

Dear Agnes, what would I do without you? you always listen to my problems and give me such good advice.

AFTER LEAVING SCHOOL, I PLANNED A TRIP TO YARMOUTH. THE FIRST NIGHT OF MY JOURNEY, I STAYED IN LONDON WHERE TO MY AMAZEMENT I MET -- STEERFORTH!

Steerforth! Don't you remember me?

My God! It's little Copperfield! Of course I remember you. Are you staying here too?

WE CHATTED OVER A GLASS OF WINE.

I've just come from Canterbury. I have been adopted by my aunt and have just finished my education. And you?

I'm at Oxford, though I get very bored there. I'm on my way to my mother's. Why don't you come?

LATER, AT HIS HOME IN HIGHGATE ...

Mother, this is my school friend, David Copperfield.

Welcome to our home, Mr. Copperfield.

This is Miss Dartle, Mr. Copperfield.

How do you do Miss Dartle?

Miss Dartle seems very clever. What a strange scar that is upon her lip.

The fact is, I did that when we were children. She annoyed me, and I threw a hammer at her.

LATER ...

DURING THIS TIME, STEERFORTH'S SERVANT, LITTIMER, LOOKED AFTER US BOTH.

Is there anything more I can have the honour of doing for you, sir?

Nothing, thank you, Littimer.

WHEN I LEFT FOR YARMOUTH, STEERFORTH DECIDED TO COME WITH ME.

So now that we're here, Copperfield, when shall we visit Mr. Peggotty and his family?

This evening would be a good time. We'll surprise them. But first, I want to see Peggotty.

BUT AT PEGGOTTY'S COTTAGE, MR. BARKIS, ALAS, WAS NOT WELL.

Do you remember what you told me, Master Davy, about Peggotty's good cooking? It was true, true as turnips!

I remember very well. Of course it was the truth.

LATER, STEERFORTH AND I WALKED ACROSS THE SANDS TO MR. PEGGOTTY'S BOAT.

If this ain't the brightest night of my life. Ham and Emily are to be married!

Ham, I give you joy, my good man. Here's my hand upon it.

Everyone likes Steerforth. He has a way with people.

That Ham is rather a thick sort of fellow for that sweet, lively girl, isn't he?

That is very unfair. Ham is a kind, decent man.

LATER, AS STEERFORTH AND I WALKED BACK TO THE HOTEL, HE SAID ...

WE PASSED BY THE SEA. A BOAT WAS TIED UP – A CLIPPER.

There she is. I've bought her. She is to be painted and newly rigged. Littimer will come and supervise. I'm changing her name – to the 'Little Emily' – and Mr. Peggotty will be master of her when I'm not here.

Now I understand! You have bought the boat to help Mr. Peggotty. How kind you are.

WHEN WE WERE HAVING DINNER THAT NIGHT, STEERFORTH HAD A STRANGE GUEST.

Miss Mowcher!

You're a fine fellow. You'd be bald but for me. So, are there any pretty women in this town?

There is one, isn't there, Copperfield?

She is as good as she is pretty. And she is engaged to be married, to a most worthy man.

Well, my flower! So far away from home! Up to mischief, I'll be bound. I've come to do your hair, as usual.

To me she seems to be throwing herself away. She was born to be a lady.

I wish he'd stop talking about Emily in that way.

31

THAT NIGHT WHEN I GOT BACK
TO PEGGOTTY'S...

Ham, what's going on? Is Emily in there?

She's talking to someone – a young woman who's got a bad reputation in Yarmouth.

Em'ly, Em'ly, please, please, take pity on me. I was once like you, but now I am disgraced.

Martha wants to go to London, to get a fresh start where no-one knows her.

Here, use this. Everything I own is yours.

I shouldn't take your money, Ham, but thank you.

Is this enough?

More than enough, thank you. Thank you. Thank you and bless you.

THE NEXT DAY, STEERFORTH AND I LEFT FOR LONDON. LITTIMER STAYED BEHIND.

Does Littimer stay here long?

We'll see. He knows what he has to do, and he'll do it.

FEW DAYS LATER, I MET AUNT BETSEY IN LONDON TO TALK ABOUT MY FUTURE.

Trot, I want you to study to be a proctor. A proctor is a lawyer with special responsibilities. I think you would do well.

Isn't the training very expensive, Aunt?

It will cost a thousand pounds.

Are you sure you can afford so much money?

Trot you are my adopted child and you have always been a credit to me. And you will be a loving son to me in my old age.

Of course I will, Aunt. Of course.

THE NEXT DAY, AS WE WENT TO DOCTORS' COMMONS WHERE I WAS TO DO MY TRAINING ...

You step into a shop, Aunt Betsey, I'll get rid of this fellow.

No, I must go with him. Get me a coach and wait for me in St. Paul's churchyard.

COMPLETELY BEWILDERED, I DID AS I WAS TOLD.

AFTER A WHILE, AUNT BETSEY RETURNED AND WE WENT TO DOCTORS' COMMONS. SHE GAVE NO EXPLANATION OF THE STRANGE INCIDENT.

So, Mr. Copperfield, you are thinking of entering our profession? There happens to be a vacancy here.

And the fee is a thousand pounds?

Which I will pay, Mr. Spenlow.

David, this is the landlady, Mrs, Crupp. She will clean the rooms and cook for you.

Yes, sir. I'll look after you.

AUNT BETSEY HAD EVEN FOUND ME FURNISHED ROOMS NEARBY.

I say, young Copperfield, are you alright?

Remember, Trot, I want you to be firm and self-reliant. Firm and self-reliant.

I will do my best, Aunt.

Never berrer.

A FEW NIGHTS LATER, I INVITED STEERFORTH AND TWO OF HIS FRIENDS TO DINE WITH ME.

THOUGH WE WERE ALL VERY DRUNK, WE DECIDED TO GO TO THE THEATRE. AND THERE ...

Agnesh! Lor bless me!

Trotwood, please go away.

Please take him home!

34

THE NEXT DAY

LATER, AT THE HOUSE WHERE SHE WAS STAYING...

Many things, small things that you have told me. I'm convinced that he is a bad influence on you.

I am worried about Father. I believe he is going to make Uriah Heep a partner in the business.

What? Uriah? That mean, fawning, cringing fellow? You must prevent it, Agnes.

He is becoming very powerful, David. If you meet him please be nice to him, for father's sake.

I'll try, but please, Agnes, don't! Don't cry, my dear sister.

THE NEXT EVENING I WAS INVITED TO DINNER. FOR THE FIRST TIME SINCE LEAVING SALEM HOUSE. I MET MY OLD FRIEND TRADDLES. UNFORTUNATELY HEEP WAS THERE TOO.

What a wonderful surprise! We must meet again soon, Traddles.

A FEW DAYS LATER, FOR AGNES'S SAKE, I INVITED HEEP TO HAVE COFFEE WITH ME.

You may have heard, Mister Copperfield, Mr. Wickfield is making me a partner in the business.

Yes. I heard something of the sort.

And, although I am an 'umble person, I love the ground my Agnes walks upon. I hope to call her mine one of these days.

I think she is above your station, Heep.

The slimy toad wants to marry Agnes!! Never! Never!

Mr. Copperfield, my daughter Dora, just returned from Paris.

How do you do Miss Spenlow?

ONE WEEKEND, MR. SPENLOW, MY SPONSOR AT DOCTORS' COMMONS, INVITED ME TO HIS HOME. AND THERE I MET HIS DAUGHTER, DORA.

And my daughter's companion, Miss Murdstone.

Mr. Copperfield and I are already aquainted, sir.

Circumstances have brought us together. I suggest we meet here as distant aquaintances.

I agree.

ONE DAY I WENT TO SEE TRADDLES...

ON RETURNING TO LONDON, I THOUGHT OF NOTHING BUT DORA.

So you see, Copperfield, I am studying law and I am engaged to be married.

I wish I were engaged – to Dora!

JUST THEN THERE WAS A KNOCK AT THE DOOR, AND IN CAME ...

Why, Mr. Micawber! I don't believe it.

Mr. and Mrs. Micawber live downstairs, I board with them.

And I am pleased to tell you that something is about to turn up!

A FEW DAYS LATER, TRADDLES, AND MR. AND MRS. MICAWBER, CAME TO DINNER. BUT OUR MEAL WAS INTERRUPTED.

What's the matter, Littimer?

Is my master here, sir? I've come from Yarmouth

No, Steerforth hasn't been here. Is the boat finished?

Yes it is, sir. I really don't know, sir. I wish you goodnight, sir.

LATER, WHEN TRADDLES AND THE MICAWBERS GOT READY TO LEAVE, I TOOK TRADDLES ASIDE.

Traddles, Mr. Micawber doesn't mean any harm, but be sure not to lend him any money.

My dear Copperfield, I haven't any money to lend.

AFTER THEY HAD ALL LEFT, I SAT BY THE FIRE, THINKING OF DORA. THEN CAME A KNOCK ON THE DOOR, AND ...

Why, here's a supper for a king! I've come from Yarmouth, and I'm starving. And I have a letter for you, from Peggotty. Barkis is very ill.

Then I must go, straightaway.

AS I WAS LEAVING, STEERFORTH SPOKE TO ME VERY SERIOUSLY ...

David, old boy, if anything should come between us, please think of me at my best.

You have no best to me, Steerforth, and no worst. You will always be my friend.

AND WE SHOOK HANDS – FOR THE LAST TIME, THOUGH I DIDN'T KNOW THAT THEN.

Barkis, my dear! Here's Master Davy. Won't you speak to Master Davy?

Barkis is willin'.

He's going out with the tide.

AND SURE ENOUGH, BARKIS WENT OUT WITH THE TIDE. HE DIED THAT NIGHT.

THERE WAS WORSE NEWS TO COME. THAT NIGHT AT MR.PEGGOTTY'S BOAT, HAM CALLED ME OUTSIDE.

Ham, what's the matter?

My love, Mas'r Davy. Em'ly, her that I would have died for - - - she's gone! Read this.

What's this? Emily's gone, and there's a man involved? Who is it?

There's been a servant about here. And a gentleman too. The gentleman named his boat the "Little Emily". I'm sorry Master Davy, but his name is Steerforth, and he's a damned villain.

Steerforth – and Littimer! How could they steal Emily away?

For the Lord's love, not Steerforth!

MR. PEGGOTTY WENT BACK INTO THE BOAT AND CAME OUT A FEW MINUTES LATER.

I SPENT THAT NIGHT AT PEGGOTTY'S ALONE. IT WAS QUITE LATE WHEN THERE CAME A KNOCK ON THE DOOR. I OPENED IT.

Where are you going, Uncle?

I'm going to seek my Em'ly. I'm going to seek my niece through all the wureld.

No, no, Dan'l! You're too upset. Wait a while.

Miss Mowcher! What is the matter? Come in.

MR. PEGGOTTY AGREED TO WAIT UNTIL THE NEXT DAY. THE TWO OF US WOULD GO TO LONDON TOGETHER.

Oh, this is terrible, Mr. Copperfield. I came as soon as I could.

When I last saw you and Steerforth, you both spoke highly of little Emily. I thought you, David, were in love with her. But it was Steerforth.

He gave me a letter, which I gave to her. I HELPED HIM IN HIS PLAN! The whole thing is my fault and now I'm here, but too late.

In a way, I helped too. I introduced him to my friends here in Yarmouth, to Emily and to Ham.

All I can tell you is that they have gone abroad. If I hear any more, I will tell you. Please, please, trust me. My small size does not mean I have a small brain. Trust me. Goodnight!

THE NEXT DAY, MR. PEGGOTTY AND I WENT TO LONDON; I TO GO BACK TO WORK, HE TO BEGIN HIS SEARCH FOR EMILY.

ALL THIS TIME I HADN'T FORGOTTEN DORA. I VISITED HER HOUSE AND GAZED AT IT FROM THE OUTSIDE.

ON MY RETURN FROM YARMOUTH, I SETTLED BARKIS' WILL FOR PEGGOTTY. I TOOK HER TO MY OFFICE AT DOCTORS' COMMONS, AND THERE WE GOT A SURPRISE!

Copperfield, you know this gentleman, I believe? Mr. Murdstone is here to get a marriage license.

Lord help the poor creature.

MR. MURDSTONE QUICKLY PAID HIS MONEY AND LEFT

You'll be glad to hear that that cross Miss Murdstone has gone to her brother's wedding. This is my friend, Julia Mills.

ONE WEEK LATER I ATTENDED MY DARLING DORA'S BIRTHDAY PARTY.

Thank you so much. What beautiful flowers.

A FEW WEEKS LATER, WE WERE ENGAGED, THOUGH WE KEPT OUR ENGAGEMENT SECRET.

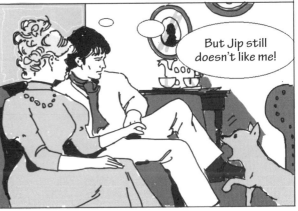

But Jip still doesn't like me!

41

THEN I GOT ANOTHER SURPRISE.

My dear Aunt! What an unexpected pleasure!

Trot, what you see here is all I have. I have lost everything. But we must get by somehow. We must carry on.

THE NEXT DAY...

David!

Agnes! Of all the people in the world, what a pleasure to see you. Please come to my rooms. Aunt Betsey is staying with me.

Your father used to advise me on money matters, Agnes, and I did very well for some years. Later, I made risky investments in banking and mining. Now I have lost everything.

And I must find work – anything

I think I have an idea. Dr. Strong, your former headmaster, has retired and lives here in London. He needs a secretary, and you always were his favourite pupil.

What an excellent idea! You always were my good angel. I'll see him tomorrow.

JUST THEN, THERE WAS A KNOCK ON THE DOOR.

That must be Father. He promised to meet me here.

Uriah Heep is active in the business, Trotwood. It's a load off my mind to have such a partner.

Your present circumstances are not what we expected, Mr. Copperfield, but it isn't only money that makes the man.

What on earth is this man about? Behave like a man, sir, not an eel!

I ACCOMPANIED AGNES AND HER FATHER BACK TO THEIR LODGINGS. AGNES AND I CHATTED LATE INTO THE NIGHT. IT WAS LIKE OLD TIMES. I TOLD HER ALL ABOUT MY WONDERFUL DORA.

Good day, Master Copperfield.

My 'umble respects, Miss Trotwood, Miss Wickfield.

THE NEXT DAY, I WENT TO SEE DR. STRONG.

So you see, I can work mornings and evenings, sir, and would be very glad of the money.

Indeed, my dear Copperfield, it would be very agreeable if you were to come and help me. Start as soon as you like. But now let us join Mrs. Strong for breakfast.

Mr. Maldon, recently returned from India. Welcome sir. Won't you join us for breakfast?

I hardly ever take breakfast, Dr. Strong. It bores me.

TO MY SURPRISE WE WERE JOINED AT BREAKFAST BY MR. JACK MALDON

As a matter of fact, I came to enquire whether Annie would like to go to the opera tonight.

You must go, Annie. You must.

I would rather not. I would much rather stay at home.

Why does Mrs. Strong look so confused? Is there something going on between her and Jack Maldon?

I PUT ASIDE MY CONCERNS ABOUT MRS. STRONG AND JACK MALDON AND WENT TO WORK FOR DR. STRONG.

And so, gentlemen, as my honourable friend has often said before, we must work for the good of the British Empire...

I ALSO REPORTED THE SPEECHES OF POLITICIANS IN PARLIAMENT.

You can earn money by making copies of legal documents. Here, try these.

Certainly, sir. With pleasure, sir

TRADDLES EVEN MANAGED TO FIND WORK FOR MR. DICK, WHO HAD VERY NEAT HANDWRITING.

ONE DAY, TRADDLES GAVE ME A LETTER FROM MR. MICAWBER.

From Mr. Micawber. It's for you.

This is an invitation to dine with the Micawbers – tonight. It seems that at long last something has Turned Up for Mr. Micawber!

Yes, my dear Copperfield, I have entered into an arrangement with our friend Uriah Heep, to be his confidential secretary.

What can Heep be up to?

I am convinced that Mr. Micawber will become a Judge or even a Chancellor.

So, may I wish you health, happiness, and success in your new career in Canterbury.

And so say I, dear friends.

DORA RETURNED TO LONDON FROM A TRIP.

Dora, I must tell you my dearest one, that I am now very poor. Could you love a beggar?

How can you ask me such a foolish question? I'll tell Jip to bite you.

Please, Dora, I'm working very hard and earning good, honest money. Is your heart still mine?

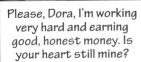

MISS MILLS JOINED US FOR TEA, AND LATER ...

I must go now, Dora. I have to get up at five o'clock in the morning to go and work for Dr. Strong.

Oh, DON'T get up at five o'clock, you naughty boy, that's ridiculous.

Yes, but stop talking about being poor and working hard. Oh, don't, don't!

Dear little Dora, I do love you so.

ONE MORNING, WHEN I ARRIVED AT WORK, DR. SPENLOW WAS WAITING FOR ME.

Copperfield, will you come with me, please?

I believe that is your writing, Mr. Copperfield?

It-it is, sir, yes.

These are also from your pen, Mr. Copperfield?

Y-y-yes, Mr. er, Spenlow.

This was a dishonourable action, Mr. Copperfield. And furthermore, it's all-nonsense! Let there be an end to it. Throw those silly love letters in the fire.

THE NEXT DAY, WHEN I WENT TO DOCTORS' COMMONS, MR. SPENLOW'S ASSISTANT WAS WAITING FOR ME.

This is a dreadful calamity, Mr. Copperfield.

Oh no, Mr. Spenlow has told everyone about Dora and me.

What is it? What's the matter?

Don't you know?

No!

Mr. Spenlow.

What about him?

He's dead!

46

Mr. Spenlow! Dead!

They found him a mile off. No one knows what happened. He lived for several hours, but never spoke again.

He was driving himself home from town in his carriage, but it arrived home without him. The reins were broken and dragging on the ground.

AFTER THIS TRAGEDY, DORA REFUSED TO SEE ANY VISITORS. SHE, JULIA MILLS, AND OF COURSE JIP WENT TO STAY WITH TWO UNMARRIED AUNTS WHO LIVED AT PUTNEY. I WAS UTTERLY MISERABLE.

ONE DAY, AUNT BETSEY SAID ...

David, you are doing nothing but mope about. I have rented out my cottage at Dover; would you please go and make sure that the new tenant is comfortable, and is paying the rent on time.

Yes, Aunt Betsey. I can stay with the Wickfields at Canterbury.

And I can tell Agnes all my troubles. She's so understanding.

BUT AT MR. WICKFIELD'S THINGS WERE MUCH CHANGED. MR. MICAWBER SHOWED ME IN.

Mr. Wickfield, where is your lovely furniture?

Oh, I don't really need it. Heep has taken over much of the business.

URIAH HEEP HAD BUILT HIMSELF A LARGE NEW OFFICE OVERLOOKING THE GARDEN.

This is very splendid, Heep. You've got most of Mr. Wickfield's furniture in here.

But I'm still very 'umble, Master Copperfield.

47

AND MRS. HEEP WAS EVERYWHERE. I HAD NO CHANCE TO SPEAK WITH AGNES ALONE. MRS. HEEP WAS ALWAYS THERE

How do you think my Uri's looking, sir?

He's looking as villainous as ever!

I see no change in him, Mrs. Heep.

Miss Agnes, let's drink to 'er 'ealth. I admire her. I adore her.

Heep! That's enough! Stop!

Look at my torturer! He has stolen my reputation, my house, and now my daughter.

If I have gone too far, I'm sorry. I can wait.

Please, please, sir, calm yourself. He has gone too far and he knows it.

I NOTICED THAT MR. WICKFIELD WAS DRINKING FAR TOO MUCH, AND URIAH HEEP WAS TAKING ADVANTAGE.

Come, sir, have another drink so that we may drink to Master Davy's 'ealth and 'appiness.

Please! No more toasts. We've all had quite enough wine.

No, I will speak out. To be her father is a privilege, but to be 'er 'usband ...

Aaagh! Never! Never! While I live!

I SPOKE TO AGNES BEFORE I LEFT THE NEXT DAY.

Dear Agnes! More than a sister. Promise me that you will not – ever – enter into a union with that man, Heep.

Bless you, David. I put my trust in God.

ONE SNOWY NIGHT, ON MY WAY HOME, I SAW A FIGURE IN A DOORWAY.

Mr. Peggotty, what are you doing here?

Mas'r Davy! It do my 'eart good to see you, sir.

WE DECIDED TO HAVE A DRINK AT A NEARBY PUB.

What are you doing here, Mr. Peggotty?

What I'm always doing. Looking for dear Emily. I'm off again tomorrow.

SUDDENLY, I NOTICED SOMEONE LISTENING TO OUR CONVERSATION. IT WAS MARTHA!

Have you heard from Emily?

Some short letters, even some money. I don't want that man Steerforth's filthy money. I'll shove it in his face some day.

The last note came from Germany, Upper Rhine. I'm off there next.

I wish you Godspeed, Mr. Peggotty. Come, I'll walk with you.

WHEN WE LEFT THE PUB, MARTHA WAS NOWHERE TO BE SEEN.

I HAD WRITTEN TO DORA'S AUNTS AT PUTNEY, ASKING IF I MIGHT PAY A CALL ON DORA. AT LAST I RECIEVED A REPLY.

Traddles, Dora's aunts have given me permission to call. Will you come with me?

With pleasure, my boy.

LATER THAT WEEK, AFTER I HAD INTRODUCED MYSELF AND TRADDLES...

My sister, Clarissa, and I are inclined to agree to your suggestion that we allow you to visit our niece.

I shall never, dear ladies, forget your kindness!

This is because we wish to have the oportunity of observing you together, over a period of time.

We shall be happy to see Mr. Copperfield to dinner every Sunday at three o'clock.

Thank you, ladies.

THEN AT LAST, JOY OF JOYS, I WAS ALLOWED TO SEE DORA.

My dearest Dora! We're to see each other every week! Your aunts have agreed.

Indeed my dear. How nice! Look! Jip has learned to stand on his hind legs.

Yes, my dear. Very clever.

But he still doesn't like me!

50

ONE DAY I TOOK AGNES TO MEET DORA AND HER AUNTS.

DORA WAS VERY NERVOUS, THINKING THAT AGNES WAS MORE CLEVER THAN SHE. IN FACT, THEY LIKED EACH OTHER IMMEDIATELY.

I am so glad that you like me. I didn't think you would. I thought you might find me silly.

I think you are charming. David is a lucky man.

AGNES WAS STAYING AT DR. STRONG'S. WHEN I TOOK HER BACK, THERE WAS A LIGHT IN THE DOCTOR'S STUDY.

Heep, what's going on?

Although I am an 'umble person, Master Copperfield, I made up my mind to tell Dr. Strong the truth: that Mrs. Strong is being unfaithful to him, with Mr. Jack Maldon.

Wickfield, is this true?

I do not know. Perhaps.

I am to blame. I married her when she was very young, thinking I could make her happy. I shall die soon, and she will be free. In the meantime, what we have said tonight is never to be said again. Come, Wickfield, help me upstairs.

You villain! How dare you speak to Dr. Strong in this way? How DARE you.

Why, Copperfield, should you strike a person that you know to be so 'umble?

You dog, I'll have no more to do with you!

AT LAST, IT WAS OFFICIAL. DORA AND I WERE TO BE MARRIED. TRADDLES' FIANCÉE, SOPHY, CAME FOR THE WEDDING.

AS DID AUNT BETSEY...

AND ALL THE REST: PEGGOTTY, THE AUNTS, MR. DICK AND MY BEAUTIFUL AGNES.

MOST OF ALL MY LOVELY BRIDE.

JIP ATE TOO MUCH WEDDING CAKE AND WAS SICK ON THE CARPET.

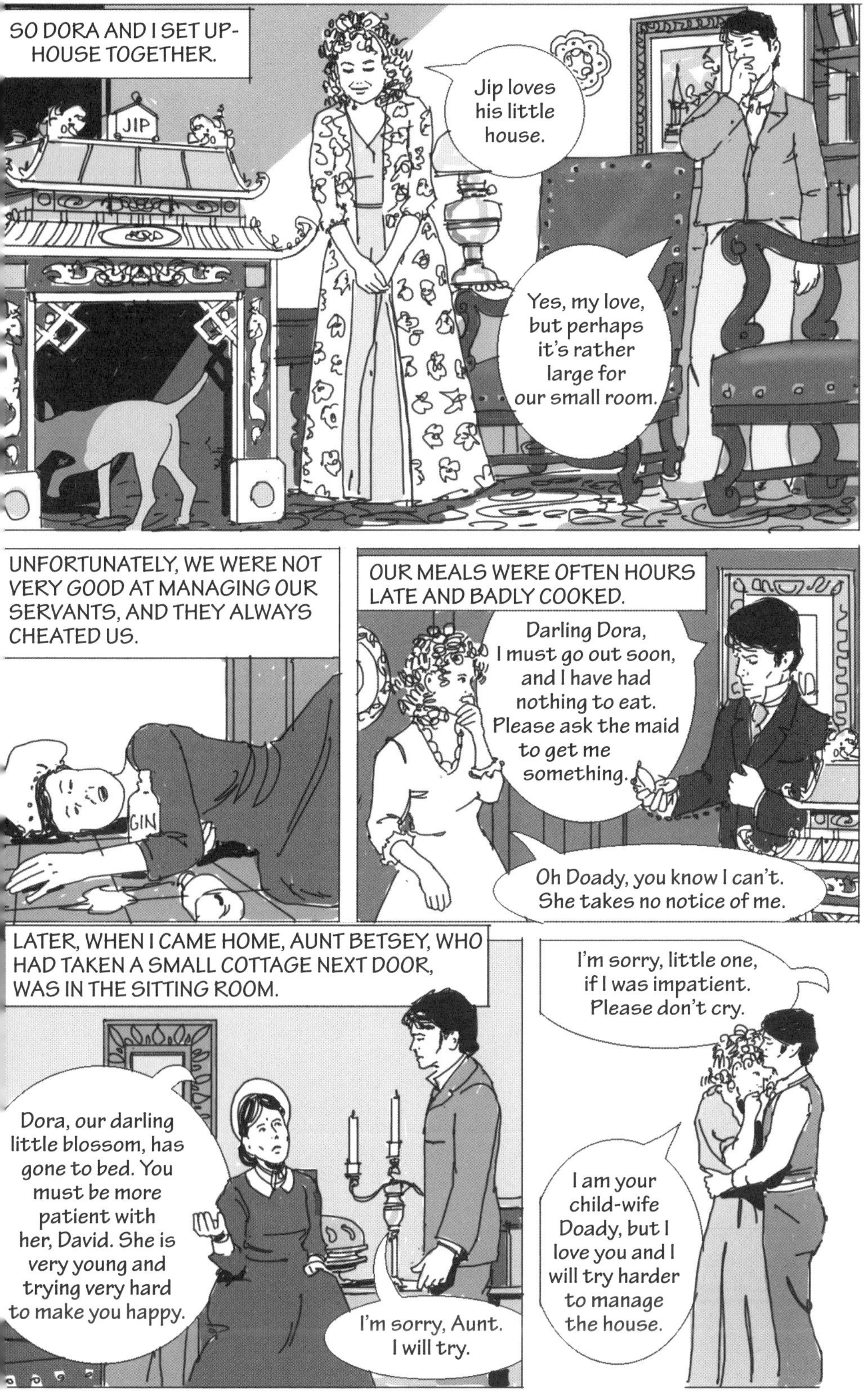
SO DORA AND I SET UP-HOUSE TOGETHER.
JIP
Jip loves his little house.
Yes, my love, but perhaps it's rather large for our small room.
UNFORTUNATELY, WE WERE NOT VERY GOOD AT MANAGING OUR SERVANTS, AND THEY ALWAYS CHEATED US.
GIN
OUR MEALS WERE OFTEN HOURS LATE AND BADLY COOKED.
Darling Dora, I must go out soon, and I have had nothing to eat. Please ask the maid to get me something.
Oh Doady, you know I can't. She takes no notice of me.
LATER, WHEN I CAME HOME, AUNT BETSEY, WHO HAD TAKEN A SMALL COTTAGE NEXT DOOR, WAS IN THE SITTING ROOM.
Dora, our darling little blossom, has gone to bed. You must be more patient with her, David. She is very young and trying very hard to make you happy.
I'm sorry, Aunt. I will try.
I'm sorry, little one, if I was impatient. Please don't cry.
I am your child-wife Doady, but I love you and I will try harder to manage the house.

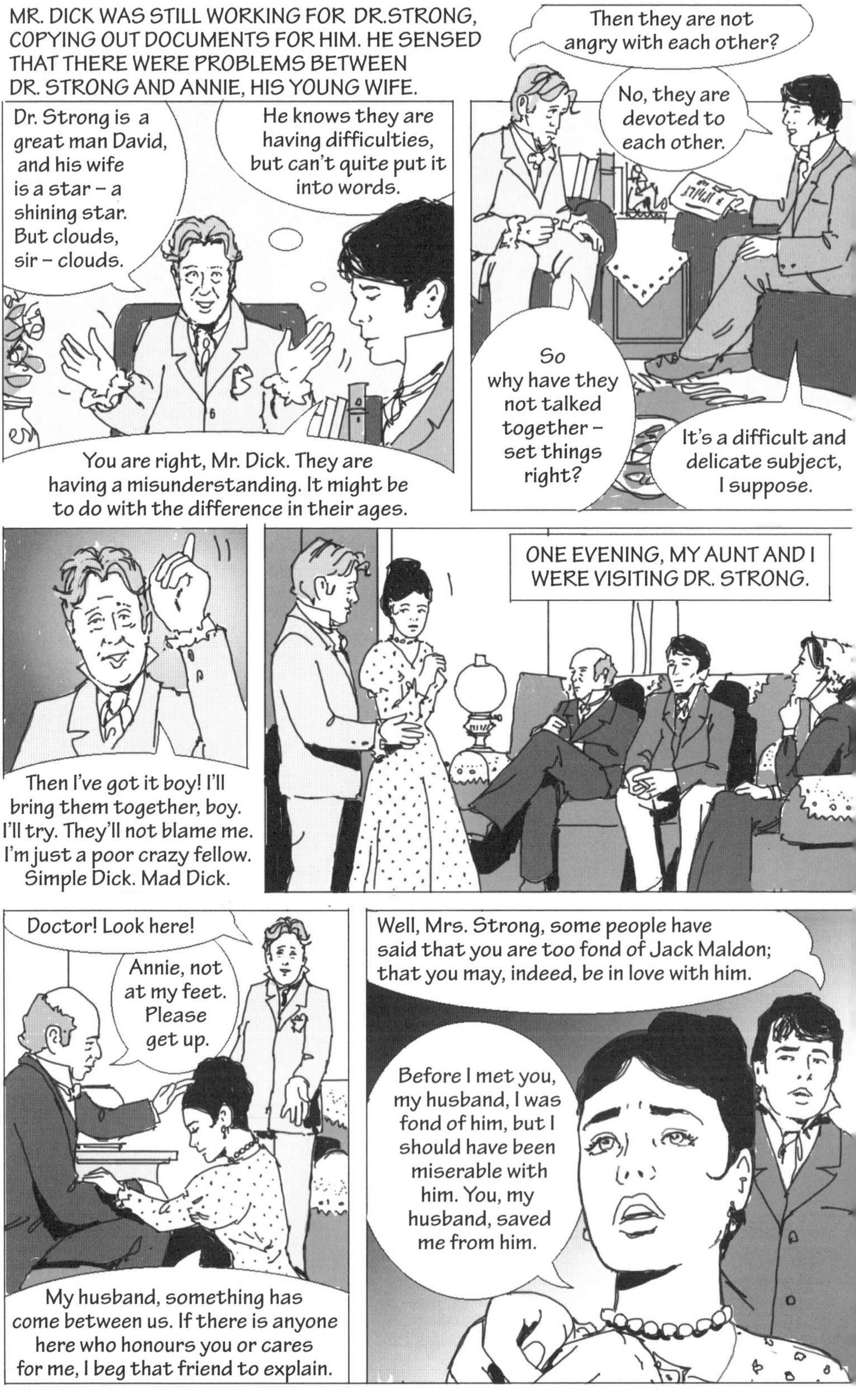
MR. DICK WAS STILL WORKING FOR DR.STRONG, COPYING OUT DOCUMENTS FOR HIM. HE SENSED THAT THERE WERE PROBLEMS BETWEEN DR. STRONG AND ANNIE, HIS YOUNG WIFE.
Dr. Strong is a great man David, and his wife is a star – a shining star. But clouds, sir – clouds.
He knows they are having difficulties, but can't quite put it into words.
You are right, Mr. Dick. They are having a misunderstanding. It might be to do with the difference in their ages.
Then they are not angry with each other?
No, they are devoted to each other.
So why have they not talked together – set things right?
It's a difficult and delicate subject, I suppose.
Then I've got it boy! I'll bring them together, boy. I'll try. They'll not blame me. I'm just a poor crazy fellow. Simple Dick. Mad Dick.
ONE EVENING, MY AUNT AND I WERE VISITING DR. STRONG.
Doctor! Look here!
Annie, not at my feet. Please get up.
My husband, something has come between us. If there is anyone here who honours you or cares for me, I beg that friend to explain.
Well, Mrs. Strong, some people have said that you are too fond of Jack Maldon; that you may, indeed, be in love with him.
Before I met you, my husband, I was fond of him, but I should have been miserable with him. You, my husband, saved me from him.

The night before Jack Maldon left for India, he tried to approach me. After all that you, my husband, had done for him! I knew then that he was wicked and ungrateful.

Oh, hold me to your heart, my husband! My love was founded on a rock, and will last forever!

Mr. Dick has foiled Heep's wicked plan to make trouble between Dr. Strong and his wife.

Annie, my pure heart! My dear girl!

ONE EVENING, I WAS GIVEN A MESSAGE. ROSA DARTLE WANTED TO SEE ME AT STEERFORTH'S HOME

I wished to speak with you because the girl has run away. Have you heard from her?

I have heard nothing.

You are a very remarkable man! And never pretend to be anything else, because I know better!

SHE LEFT ME IN THE GARDEN AND CAME BACK WITH LITTIMER, STEERFORTH'S MANSERVANT.

I tried to break the news gently. I even offered to marry her myself – I would have been good to her. But the young lady went mad – tried to kill herself. For her own good, I locked her up, but she got away and hasn't been seen since. That was in Naples, sir.

Tell him.

I travelled with Mr. Steerforth and the young woman. For a while they seemed very happy. She was admired wherever we went. But Steerforth tired of her. One day he went away leaving me to tell her that he was gone forever.

Cruel! Inhuman! I must tell her family at once. Good day to you both.

55

I KNEW WHERE MR. PEGGOTTY STAYED WHEN HE WAS IN LONDON ... QUICKLY I TOLD HIM THE NEWS.

Mas'r Davy, I have felt so sure as she was living, I have been so led by it, I don't believe I can be mistaken. No! Em'ly's alive!

Why don't we go and find Martha? Perhaps she can tell us something.

JUST IN TIME, WE FOUND MARTHA. SHE WAS ABOUT TO THROW HERSELF IN THE RIVER THAMES.

Martha! Martha! Stop it! We need you! You must help us!

The river! The river! Let me go. I just want to die.

WHEN I ARRIVED HOME I WAS SURPRISED TO SEE THAT THE DOOR OF AUNT BETSEY'S COTTAGE WAS OPEN.

Martha, we believe Em'ly is alive -- and alone. She is likely, one day, to make her lonely way back to London. Help us find her, and may heaven reward you.

Will you trust me?

Full and free!

Why, it's the man who once approached Aunt Betsey on the street. Why is she giving him money?

What is the use of this?

I can spare no more.

It'll have to do, I suppose.

Aunt, that man is frightening you again. Let me speak to him. Who is he?

My dear, good Aunt! I thought your husband was dead.

Dead to me, but living. When I married him I loved him very much, but he broke my heart and stole my money. Then he left me for another woman. You see what he is now: a tramp.

Trot, it's my husband. Come inside for a minute.

Now you know my grumpy, frumpy story, and it will be our secret, Trot.

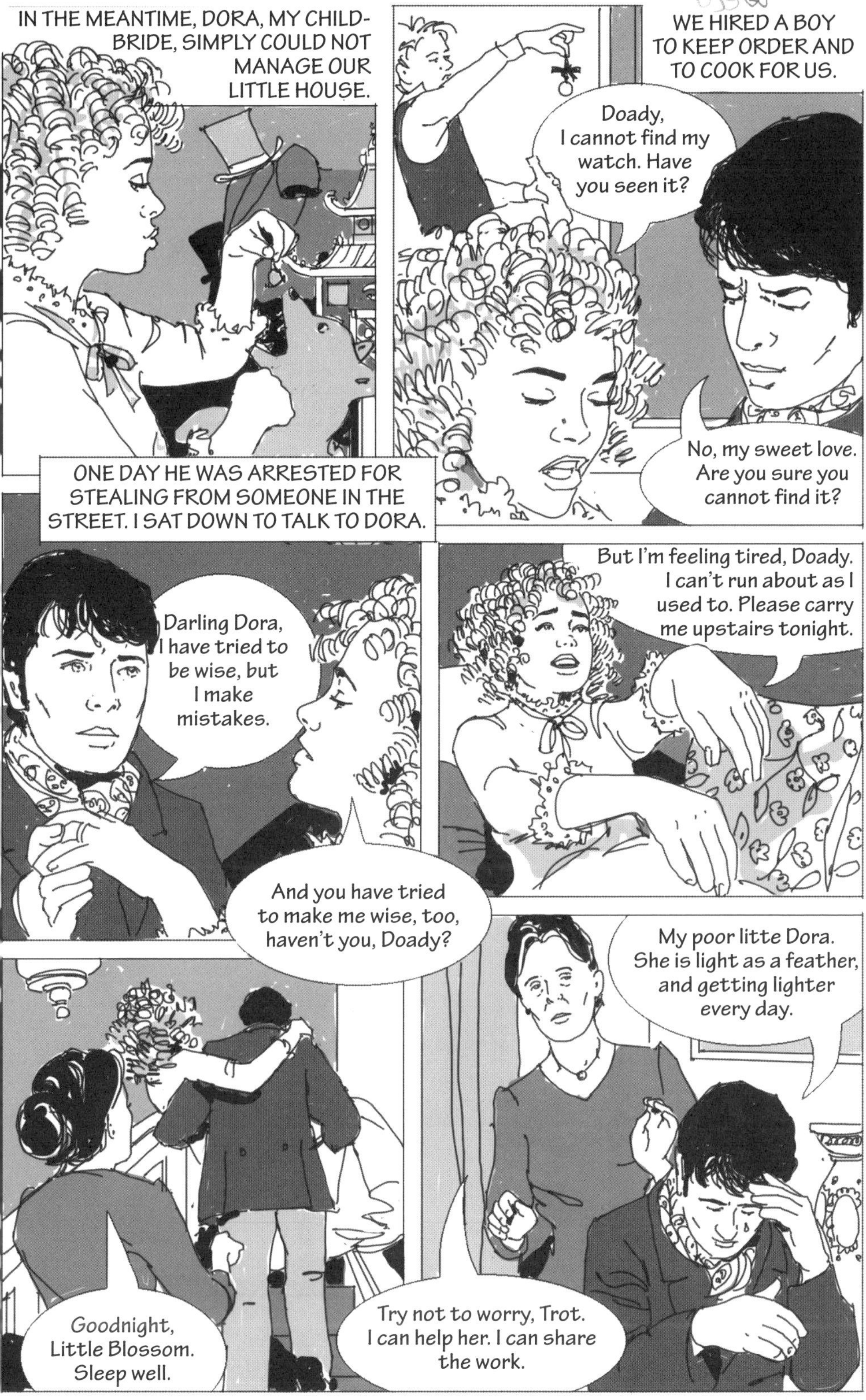

IN THE MEANTIME, DORA, MY CHILD-BRIDE, SIMPLY COULD NOT MANAGE OUR LITTLE HOUSE.
تعاونا
WE HIRED A BOY TO KEEP ORDER AND TO COOK FOR US.
Doady, I cannot find my watch. Have you seen it?
No, my sweet love. Are you sure you cannot find it?
ONE DAY HE WAS ARRESTED FOR STEALING FROM SOMEONE IN THE STREET. I SAT DOWN TO TALK TO DORA.
Darling Dora, I have tried to be wise, but I make mistakes.
And you have tried to make me wise, too, haven't you, Doady?
But I'm feeling tired, Doady. I can't run about as I used to. Please carry me upstairs tonight.
Goodnight, Little Blossom. Sleep well.
My poor litte Dora. She is light as a feather, and getting lighter every day.
Try not to worry, Trot. I can help her. I can share the work.

I say, Traddles, I've just received a letter from Mr. Micawber. He seems very upset – wants us to meet him the day after tomorrow, outside the King's Bench Prison.

And I've had a letter from Mrs. Micawber. She says he's behaving very strangely, but won't tell her what's the matter.

Come. Mr. Micawber, we can't talk here. We're invited to my aunt's. She wants you to make some of your special punch.

I'll try.

BUT LATER, AT AUNT BETSEY'S...

Poor man. He is very troubled.

It's no good - I am too upset to make punch tonight.

Please, Mr. Micawber, speak out. You are among friends.

I want to choke the eyes out of the head of that cheat and liar, HEEP! I'll say nothing – and live nowhere – until I have crushed that serpent HEEP!

WHEN MR. MICAWBER HAD CALMED DOWN. HE DEPARTED. AN HOUR LATER, WE RECEIVED A NOTE FROM HIM.

Mr. and Mrs. Micawber want us to meet them in Canterbury, one week from today. Aunt Betsey, they would especially like you to come.

And I shan't come without Mr. Dick.

THE NEXT EVENING, MARTHA ASKED ME TO GO TO LONDON WITH HER ON URGENT BUSINESS. SHE TOOK ME TO THE DISMAL HOUSE WHERE SHE LIVED.

I have asked Mr. Peggotty to come here. That's my room at the top of the stairs. But who is that going in?

I know who it is. It's Rosa Dartle.

I MOVED TO ONE SIDE, TRYING TO GET A BETTER VIEW OF THE ROOM.

I have come to see James Steerforth's fancy woman, the girl who ran away with him and is the talk of the town amongst the commonest people.

Emily!

Me? Do you mean me?

Will Mr. Peggotty never come?

There are doorways and dust heaps for women like you. Find one, and take your flight to Heaven --- or Hell.

Thank God – I hear Mr. Peggotty coming at last.

Mas'r Davy, I thank God. My dream has come true. He has guided me to my darling. I can take her home.

Oh, have mercy on me. Show me mercy, or I shall die mad!

MR. PEGGOTTY STRODE INTO THE ROOM AND TOOK EMILY INTO HIS ARMS ROSA DARTLE RAN OUT OF THE ROOM.

59

EARLY THE NEXT MORNING, MR. PEGGOTTY CAME TO SEE AUNT BETSEY AND MYSELF.

I want to tell you Em'ly's story, Mas'r Davy, Miss Trotwood, it's this: when Steerforth left her, she ran away from his servant. She ran away in the middle of the night.

But she was in a foreign country – Italy.

Uncle! Uncle! Where are you? Help me!

A kindly woman her own age took pity on her and took her in.

At last, she made her way back to London – young, pretty, and not a penny in the world. Luckily, Martha found her.

And as to the future, good friend, what now?

Emily, come with me. Your uncle loves you and forgives you. Come. He is waiting.

There's mighty countries – far from here. We will begin a new life over in Australia. No one there will know Emily's past.

MR. PEGGOTTY AND I WENT TO YARMOUTH. HE WANTED TO CLOSE UP THE BOAT AND SAY HIS FAREWELLS. HAM HAD DECIDED TO STAY IN YARMOUTH, IN THE COTTAGE HE HAD BUILT FOR EMILY.

Please tell Emily that I'm alright. I shall never forget her, and will remember her in my prayers.

And I'll take good care of Ham, the best boatman on the coast.

WE ALL TOOK THE COACH BACK TO LONDON, WHERE EMILY, MR. PEGGOTTY, AND SARAH GUMMIDGE WOULD BOARD THE SHIP TO AUSTRALIA.

I'm so glad you agreed to let me come to Australia. It will be a new start, for all of us.

While I'm in London I'll make sure that Martha is taken care of.

We must all help her.

IT WAS TIME FOR TRADDLES AND I TO KEEP OUR APPOINTMENT WITH MR. MICAWBER IN CANTERBURY.

Aunt, you must go with Doady and Traddles. Mr. Micawber wants you there, Why shouldn't you both go?

Why, what a question! But you know, Blossom, you can't do without me.

You'll only be gone one night, and Jip will take care of me while you are gone. Doady will carry me upstairs before you go, and I won't come down again until you come back.

TO THIS WE ALL AGREED.

WHEN WE GOT TO CANTERBURY, WE MET MICAWBER AT MR. WICKFIELD'S HOUSE.

This is an unexpected pleasure. Micawber, please fetch Miss Agnes – and my mother.

Go along, Micawber. Don't hang about. I recommend that you take yourself off.

No – sir. I-choose-to-stay!

61

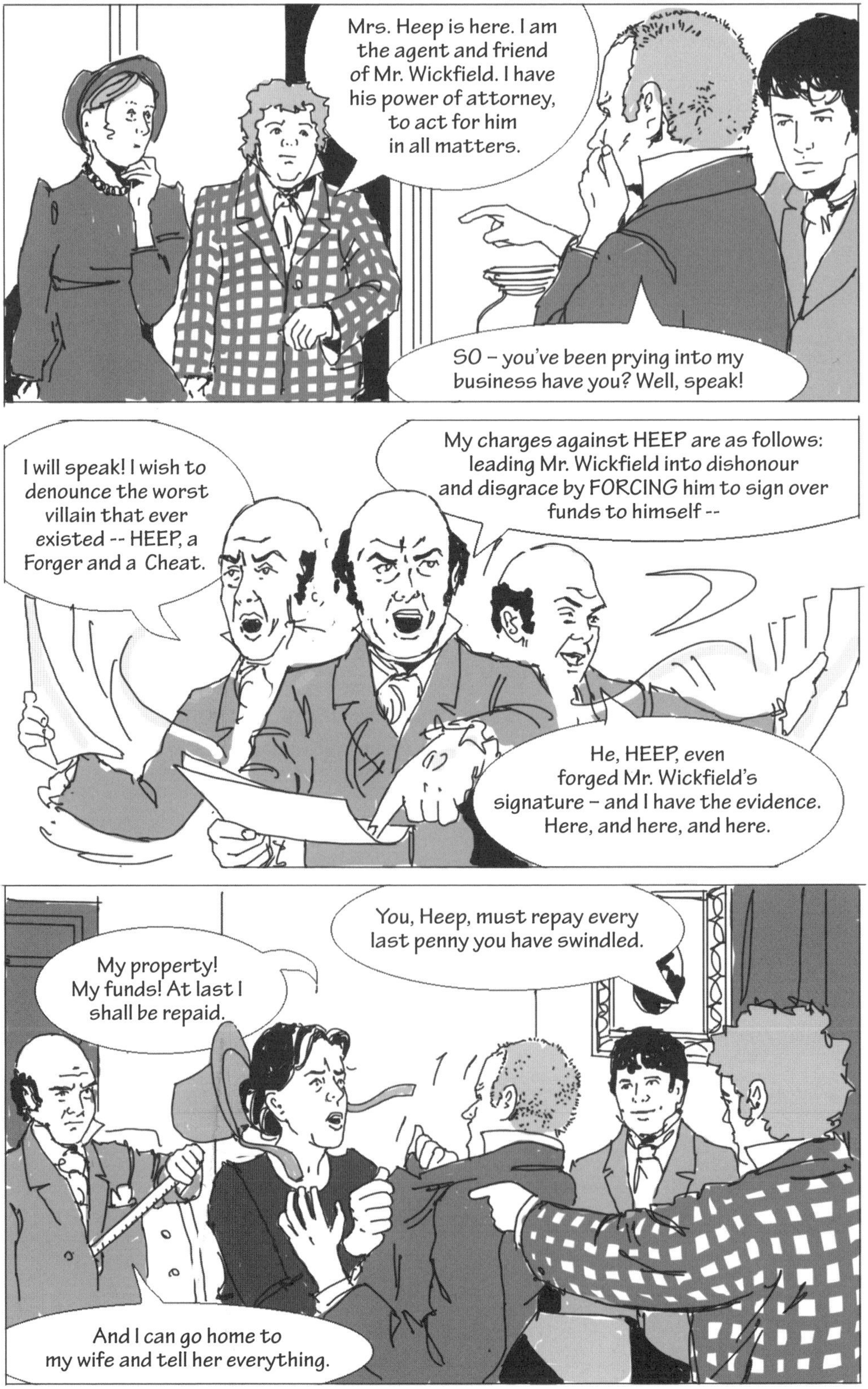
Mrs. Heep is here. I am the agent and friend of Mr. Wickfield. I have his power of attorney, to act for him in all matters.
SO – you've been prying into my business have you? Well, speak!
I will speak! I wish to denounce the worst villain that ever existed -- HEEP, a Forger and a Cheat.
My charges against HEEP are as follows: leading Mr. Wickfield into dishonour and disgrace by FORCING him to sign over funds to himself --
He, HEEP, even forged Mr. Wickfield's signature – and I have the evidence. Here, and here, and here.
My property! My funds! At last I shall be repaid.
You, Heep, must repay every last penny you have swindled.
And I can go home to my wife and tell her everything.

Mr Micawber, with your large family, have you ever thought of emigrating? To Australia, for example?

Well, sir, you have helped me to get my money back. I should be delighted to provide the money for your travel.

And for my part, Miss Trotwood, I will guarantee to repay it, every penny! I am convinced, my dear madam, that it is the land, the only land, for me and my family.

Madam, it was the dream of my youth, but I've never been able to raise the money to go.

And in Australia, my dear Wilkins, something is sure to Turn Up!

AND SO IT WAS DECIDED.

BUT SADLY WHEN I RETURNED HOME, MY SWEET DORA WAS EVEN WEAKER THAN BEFORE.

You look so lovely, my darling. Aunt Betsey takes wonderful care of you.

Oh, Doady, I do love you – poor stupid little me. Please, please, could you send for Agnes? I do so want to see her.

AGNES OF COURSE CAME AT ONCE. SHE WENT UPSTAIRS TO SEE DORA. I SAT ALONE WITH JIP.

Jip, Jip, I am afraid. She is very, very ill.

Jip-Jip-- stiff and cold. Not you!

David, I'm so sorry. It is over. She has slipped away.

No! No! I can't bear it! NO! And Jip is dead too. He died this very moment.

IN SPITE OF OUR GRIEF, AUNT BETSEY AND I HAD TO RETURN TO CANTERBURY WHERE TRADDLES AND MR MICAWBER WERE SORTING OUT MR. WICKFIELD'S AFFAIRS.

Mr. Micawber is working tirelessly to help straighten out the mess left by Heep. Mr. Dick, too. He kept an eye on the Heeps until they were taken away to prison.

Now he's looking after Mr. Wickfield.

I always said Dick was a remarkable man, didn't I, Trot?

The good news is that Mr. Wickfield will be able to settle with his clients and retire in peace, though Agnes may have to sell the house.

Let us speak with her.

Agnes, we have proved your father's innocence, and Heep is repaying the missing funds. But you will need a small income. You may have to sell the house.

I think not. I have been giving it some thought. I should like to keep a school. It's good, useful work, and I will be able to look after father.

An excellent idea, my dear.

I am pleased to tell you that I am now in a position to pay your debts, plus the fares for your family to Australia where you will begin a new life and never, never get into debt again, Mr. Micawber.

No, ma'am. I promise.

AUNT BETSEY SPOKE AGAIN WITH MR. MICAWBER.

FOR SOME TIME, AUNT BETSEY HAD SEEMED TO BE UPSET ABOUT SOMETHING. ON OUR RETURN FROM LONDON, SHE EXPLAINED ...

Ashes to ashes, dust to dust...

Trotwood, I told you some time ago about my husband. He has been in hospital these past weeks, and died two days ago. Before he died, he apologised for all the sadness he has caused me.

A FEW DAYS LATER, MR PEGGOTTY BROUGHT ME A LETTER. EMILY WISHED ME TO TAKE IT TO HAM.

He was a fine-looking man when I married him, Trot. May he rest in peace.

She has written to thank Ham for his kind words, which have given her some peace of mind. And she says goodbye---forever.

THE NEXT DAY, I WENT TO YARMOUTH TO GIVE HAM THE NOTE AS REQUESTED.

Look at those black clouds over Yarmouth. A great storm is on its way.

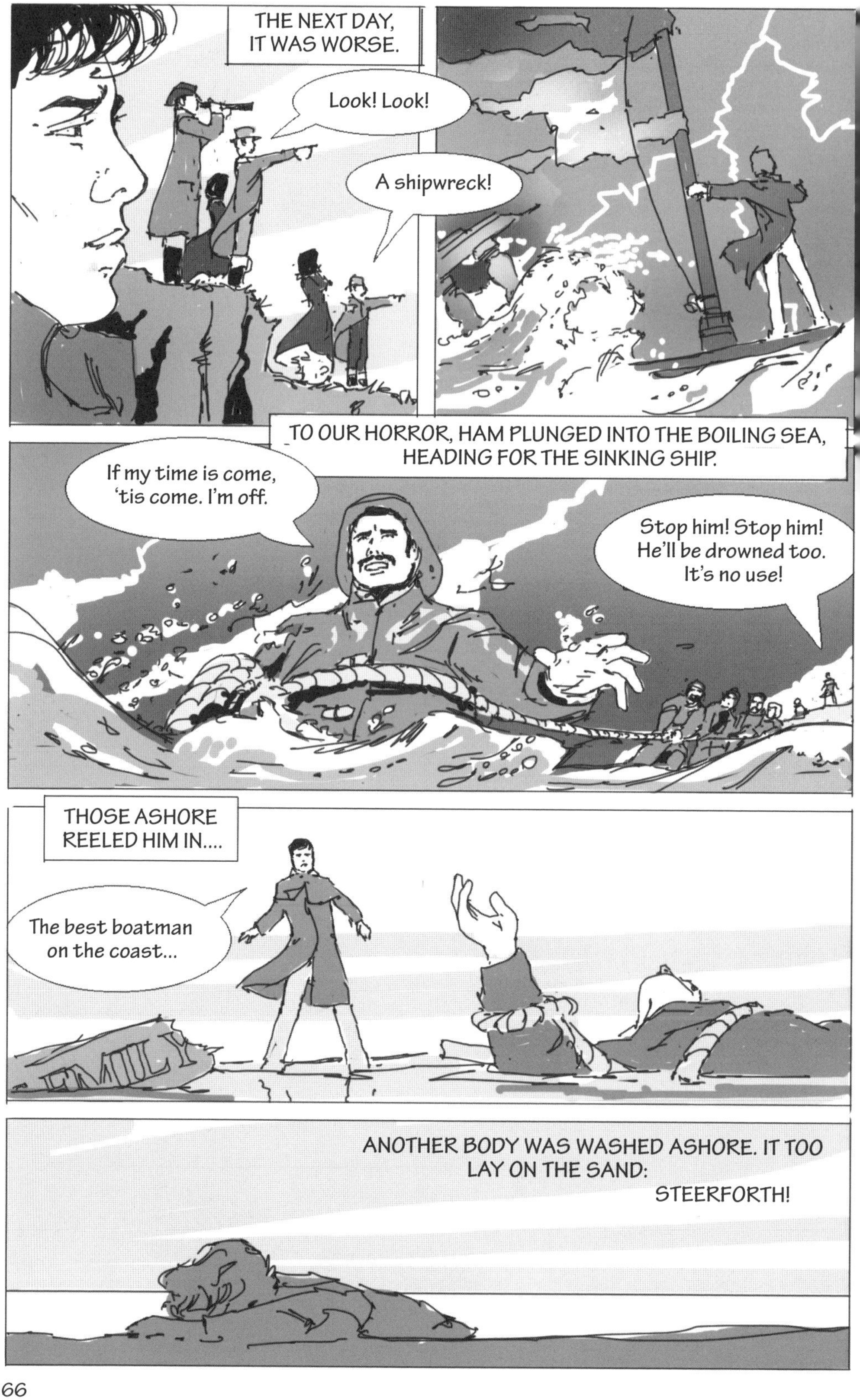
THE NEXT DAY, IT WAS WORSE.
Look! Look!
A shipwreck!
TO OUR HORROR, HAM PLUNGED INTO THE BOILING SEA, HEADING FOR THE SINKING SHIP.
If my time is come, 'tis come. I'm off.
Stop him! Stop him! He'll be drowned too. It's no use!
THOSE ASHORE REELED HIM IN....
The best boatman on the coast...
EMILY
ANOTHER BODY WAS WASHED ASHORE. IT TOO LAY ON THE SAND:
STEERFORTH!

Mrs Steerforth, Miss Dartle, I have very bad news. He is dead--drowned.

Oh, oh! My boy, my son.

This is YOUR OWN FAULT. YOU brought him up to be what he was--- SELFISH.

Please, please, Miss Dartle. Think of his mother's feelings.

LATER, WHEN I LEFT, MRS STEERFORTH HAD BEEN PUT TO BED. SHE LAY LIKE A STATUE, NEVER MOVING.

STEERFORTH LAY IN A NEARBY ROOM, WHERE I SAID GOODBYE TO HIM---FOREVER.

Ham died tragically but bravely in a terrible storm, trying to rescue someone from a shipwreck. It maybe in the newspapers. It's better Mr. Peggotty and Emily do not learn of it. Please make sure they are not told.

BACK IN TOWN, I HAD A QUIET WORD WITH MR. MICAWBER.

Yes, of course. In any case, we are to be aboard our ship before seven tomorrow morning.

67

I will drink all happiness and success to you, Mr. and Mrs. Micawber, with pleasure.

And I, too.

And Peggotty and I will come to wave goodbye at Gravesend tomorrow.

THAT NIGHT, MR MICAWBER INVITED US ALL TO JOIN HIM AND HIS FAMILY FOR A GREAT BOWL OF PUNCH.

SO THE NEXT MORNING...

Oh, Peggotty, look, there's Emily, and Martha too, and Sarah Gummidge. They'll all make a fresh start.

God bless them, God bless them all.

AFTER THE EMIGRANTS HAD LEFT FOR AUSTRALIA, AUNT BETSEY RETURNED TO HER COTTAGE AT DOVER. I DECIDED TO GO TRAVELLING, HOPING TO ESCAPE THE SADNESS OF LOSING DORA.

Here, sir. These are for you.

SOME MONTHS LATER, I WAS GIVEN A PACKET OF LETTERS.

Thank you, madame.

Darling Agnes, some news of her, but all her thoughts are of me: sympathy at my loss, pride in my achievements, confidence that I shall do more.

AGNES' LETTER GAVE ME COURAGE. I DECIDED TO WRITE A BOOK.

Perhaps Traddles will be able to find a publisher willing to publish my book.

GRADUALLY, I REALISED THAT MY FEELINGS FOR AGNES WERE CHANGING. SHE WAS BECOMING VERY DEAR TO ME. I WANTED HER TO BE MINE, BUT IT WAS TOO LATE.

SOME MONTHS LATER...

It's from the publishers. My book is doing very well. Dear Agnes, I did it for her.

THREE YEARS PASSED BEFORE I RETURNED TO LONDON. TRADDLES HAD MOVED INTO PROPER LEGAL CHAMBERS, THE INNS OF COURT. I WENT TO SEE HIM.

My dearest Copperfield! How glad I am to see you! But you've missed the ceremony.

What ceremony?

Why the marriage ceremony. I am married! To the dearest girl in the world. David, my wife!

From the bottom of my heart, I wish you all the joy in the world.

LATER I SAT IN FRONT OF THE FIRE AT THE INN WHERE I WAS STAYING. ALL I COULD THINK ABOUT WAS AGNES.

Perhaps I will never again have a wife and home. I know Agnes loves me, but like a sister. She's sure to marry someone else.

THE NEXT DAY, I WENT TO DOVER TO SEE MY AUNT AND PEGGOTTY!

I'm now your aunt's housekeeper, Master Davy, and I'm very happy here.

And when, Trot, when are you going to Canterbury to see Agnes?

Tomorrow evening, Aunt. Will you come with me?

No, thank you. I shall stay where I am.

Has Agnes a---any lover?

Plenty! She could have married twenty times since you have been gone. But I think she has an attachment, Trot. I think she has loved someone for a very long time.

THE NEXT EVENING, I SAW MY DARLING AGNES.
SHE PLAYED THE PIANO FOR HER FATHER
AND ME, JUST LIKE IN THE OLD DAYS.

I must hide my altered feelings. She loves me like a brother, that is all.

FOR THE NEXT FEW MONTHS I STAYED AT MY AUNT'S HOUSE FINISHING MY LATEST BOOK.

MY BOOKS WERE BECOMING FAMOUS. I RECEIVED MANY LETTERS FROM MY READERS, INCLUDING ONE FROM MR CREAKLE, FORMER HEADMASTER OF SALEM HOUSE!

I say Traddles, I've had a letter from Mr Creakle. Remember how he used to beat you for drawing skeletons? It seems he is now a Magistrate and in charge of a prison. He would like me to see his prison. Would you like to come?

I don't object.

Ah, Copperfield, Traddles, very good of you to come. Let me show you round.

Here he is, Number Twenty-Seven, our model prisoner. How are you today?

I am very 'umble, sir!

It's Heep!

I am changed since I come here. There's evil everywhere, but I forgive you all. I pity all who ain't brought here.

71

I WAS ABOUT TO LEAVE TO SEE AGNES AGAIN.

Trot...

Yes, Aunt?

I think Agnes is going to be married.

Then God bless her.

WHEN I SAW AGNES, I WENT STRAIGHT TO THE POINT. I HAD TO KNOW...

Agnes, please tell me your secret. Let me share it. If you love someone, please tell me.

Trotwood, I will speak to you by and by – another time. Don't ask me now. Don't! Don't!

Agnes, you're crying. I can't bear it. The truth is, I went away, loving you. I stayed away, loving you. I returned home -- loving you. Thinking you loved someone else, I've been afraid to tell you.

And I have loved you all my life.

TWO WEEKS LATER, WE WERE MARRIED.

I told you Agnes was going to be married.

TEN YEARS WENT QUICKLY BY – BUSY, HAPPY YEARS. ONE EVENING...

Someone to see you, sir. An old man. He looks like a farmer.

Please show him in.

Mr Peggotty!

MR PEGGOTTY GAVE US ALL THE NEWS FROM AUSTRALIA.

We all worked hard, Mas'r Davy, and we have all done well. Em'ly mostly helps others – looking after the sick, taking care of other people's children.

She learned of Ham's death from an old newspaper belonging to a traveller from Norfolk.

She was very sad, and very quiet, for months afterwards.

Is Martha still with you?

Martha got married to a young farm-worker. They live far away, but I hear they're very happy.

And Sarah Gummidge?

A ship's cook who had decided to become a farmer asked her to marry him. But Sarah Gummidge picked up a bucket and beat him about the head! So that was that.

And Mr Micawber? He has paid off all his debts here – to my Aunt, even to Traddles.

Wilkins Micawber, Esquire, is now a Magistrate! Oh, yes, he is often in the newspapers. He is a highly respected citizen.

73

AND NOW, MY WRITTEN STORY ENDS. I THINK OF THOSE WHO HAVE HELPED ME ON MY WAY. MY AUNT IS OVER EIGHTY YEARS OLD, BUT STILL WALKS SIX MILES A DAY, EVEN IN WINTER....

DEAR PEGGOTTY, MY *GOOD OLD* NURSE, IS NEVER WITHOUT HER SEWING.

MR. DICK LOVES TO TEACH MY CHILDREN TO FLY KITES.

AND ONE DAY TRADDLES WILL BE A JUDGE.

You will be glad to hear that I shall finish the Memorial very soon. Your aunt is the most extraordinary woman in the world, sir.

BUT
ONE FACE SHINES ON ME LIKE A HEAVENLY LIGHT –

AGNES,

TO MY LIFE'S END.

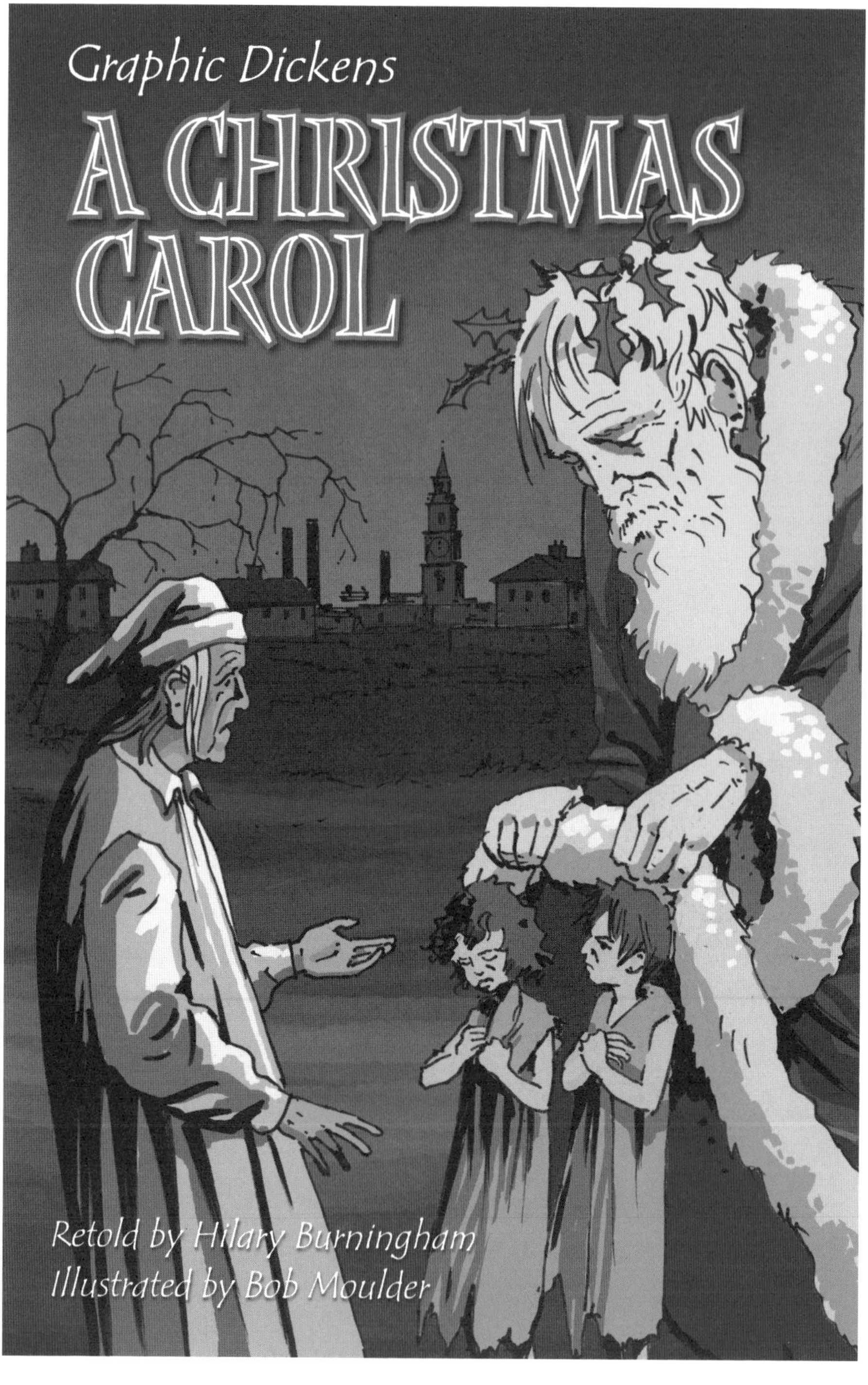
Graphic Dickens
A CHRISTMAS CAROL
Retold by Hilary Burningham
Illustrated by Bob Moulder

ISBN: 978 1 78322 013 7

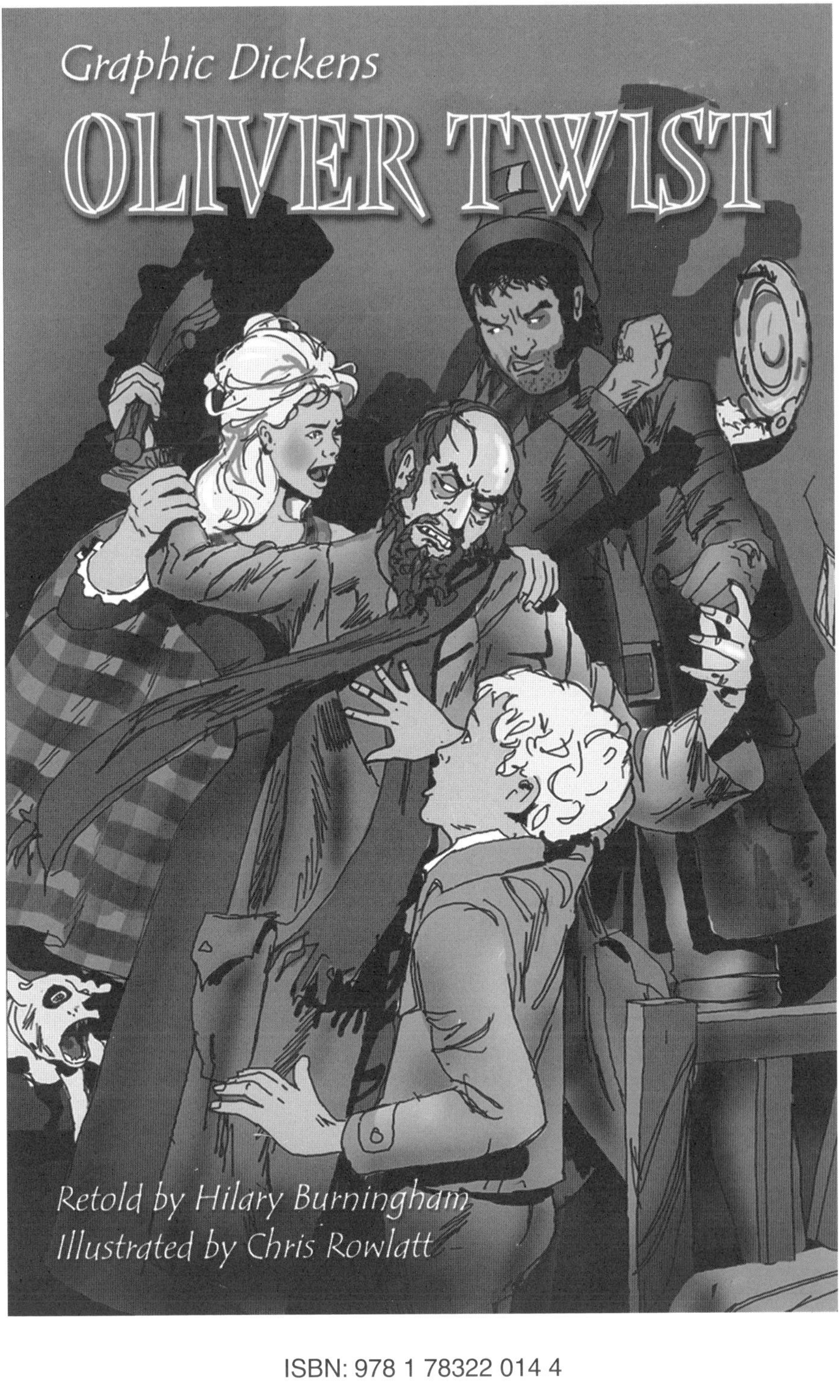
Graphic Dickens
OLIVER TWIST
Retold by Hilary Burningham
Illustrated by Chris Rowlatt

ISBN: 978 1 78322 014 4

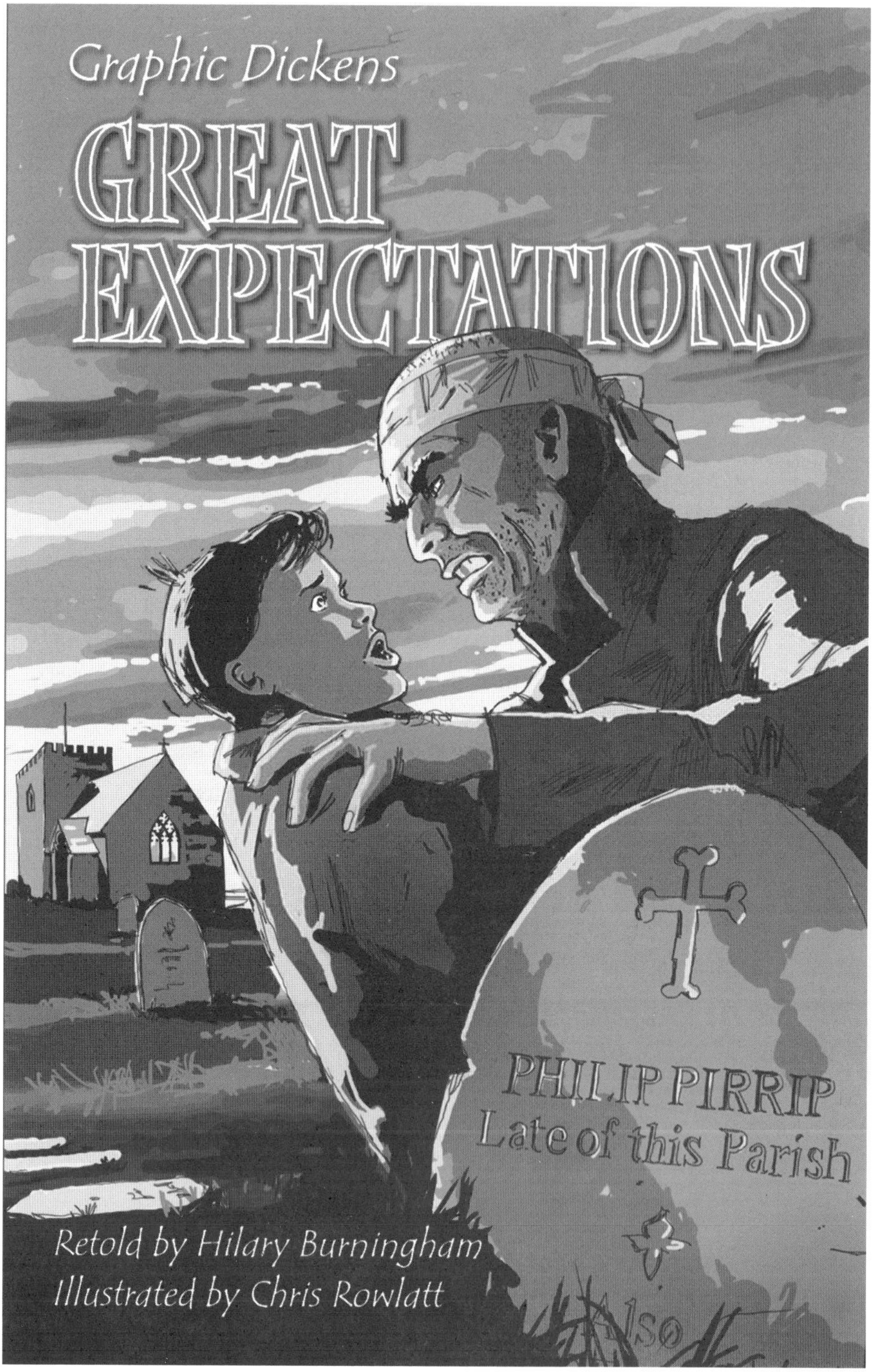
Graphic Dickens
GREAT EXPECTATIONS
PHILIP PIRRIP
Late of this Parish
Also
Retold by Hilary Burningham
Illustrated by Chris Rowlatt

ISBN: 978 1 78322 015 1